HUNTED

OUTRUN. OUTLAST. OUTWIT.

Thrilling Tales

Edited By Sarah Waterhouse

First published in Great Britain in 2020 by:

Young Writers
Remus House
Coltsfoot Drive
Peterborough
PE2 9BF
Telephone: 01733 890066
Website: www.youngwriters.co.uk

Printed and bound in the UK by BookPrintingUK
Website: www.bookprintinguk.com
YB0435M

FOREWORD

IF YOU'VE BEEN SEARCHING FOR EPIC ADVENTURES, TALES OF SUSPENSE AND IMAGINATIVE WRITING THEN SEARCH NO MORE! YOUR HUNT IS AT AN END WITH THIS ANTHOLOGY OF MINI SAGAS.

We challenged secondary school students to craft a story in just 100 words. In this first installment of our SOS Sagas, their mission was to write on the theme of 'Hunted'. But they weren't restricted to just predator vs prey, oh no. They were encouraged to think beyond their first instincts and explore deeper into the theme.

The result is a variety of styles and genres and, as well as some classic cat and mouse games, inside these pages you'll find characters looking for meaning, people running from their darkest fears or maybe even death itself on the hunt.

Here at Young Writers it's our aim to inspire the next generation and instill in them a love for creative writing, and what better way than to see their work in print? The imagination and skill within these pages are proof that we might just be achieving that aim! Well done to each of these fantastic authors.

So if you're ready to find out if the hunter will become the hunted, read on!

CONTENTS

Connor Nash (13)	52
Dominic Hampshire (13)	53
James Alexander Douglas Atkins (14)	54
Alex Impey (15)	55
Euan James Aspey (14)	56
Amber Johns (14)	57
Olivia Ormsby (13)	58
Lily-Grace Riley (14)	59
Daniel Wilde (14)	60
Dylan James Ferris (13)	61
Finton Jay Kilbey (13)	62
Harry Hughes (13)	63
Alexa Hewitt (13)	64
Emily Drake (13)	65
Matty Watton	66
Amber Davis (15)	67
Francesca Hayward (14)	68
Sophie Webb (15)	69
Ruby Gould (14)	70
Nichola Davenhill (13)	71
Chloe Mills (15)	72
Nathan Warner (14)	73
Bethany Pye (13)	74
Grace Campbell (14)	75
Brook Maiden (13)	76
Poppy Risdale (13)	77
Grace Stewart (13)	78
Jack Oliver Sanders (13)	79
Rhys Christopher Ayres (13)	80
Matt Carter (14)	81
Sam Livingstone (13)	82
Megan Bradley (14)	83
Max Seadon (15)	84
Jamie Beeson (14)	85
Fletcher Ford (13)	86
Lilly Myler (13)	87
Ashleigh May Louth (15)	88
Jay Merrett (14)	89
William Jarvis (13)	90
Sam Spear (13)	91
Jake Walding (13)	92
Joshua Neal (14)	93

Carmen West (13)	94
Leah Saunders (13)	95
Mason Rimmer (13)	96
Natasha Powell (13)	97
Scarlett Begley (13)	98
Ben Powell (13)	99
Kiera Brennan (14)	100

The Meadows School, Dove Holes

Chelsea Terry (15)	101

The Roseland Academy, Tregony

Phoebe Nel (12)	102
Erin Sylvia Gilmour (11)	103
Ariane Trewinnard (12)	104
Evie Howard (11)	105
Evie-Mae Arthur (12)	106
Ryan Marshall (14)	107
Maisie Coombe-Gollop (11)	108
Elena Grace Waugh (13)	109
Luke Montagu (11)	110
Leo McGovern	111
Fintan Lawler (12)	112
Ellie Hancock (13)	113
Harry Frederick Lutey (13)	114
Oliver John Gray (11)	115
Lilah Courage (12)	116
Hannah Gulliver (11)	117
Tremayne Richards (11)	118
Charlotte Gray (12)	119
Jenna Ashley Cooper (11)	120
Chloe Edwards (11)	121
Brody Gibson (13)	122
Brandon Garrett (11)	123
Lochlainn Finn Lönze (11)	124
Lily Miller (13)	125
Amelia Wykes (12)	126
Toby Milnes (12)	127
Zenna Martin (12)	128
Sophie Kent (12)	129
Jemima Hetherington (12)	130

Harry Gildersleeve (12)	131
Sarah Mitchell (12)	132
Lily Rose Boboefe (12)	133
Charlie Wheeler	134
Amelia Harrington (12)	135
Skyeanne Nash (13)	136
Lily Jones (12)	137
Adam Clow (13)	138
Alfie Alexander Heslip (12)	139
Thomas Edwards (11)	140
Yumi Storey (12)	141
Fia Brunton (11)	142
Olivia Rees-Challis (12)	143
Daisy Thomas (12)	144
Phoebe Sophia Emmett (12)	145
Theo Schofield (13)	146
Callum Knight (14)	147
Maddi Sophia Kent-Fuller (13)	148
Megan Richards (12)	149
Chloe Enfield (12)	150
Macey Rodda (11)	151
Bethany Champion (12)	152
Alfie Lambirth (11)	153
Niamh Star Burnett (13)	154
Sophia Tame (13)	155
Lucas Burton (12)	156
Jacob White (13)	157
Caera Dye (11)	158
Ella Wheildon (11)	159
Keala Harrington (12)	160
Matilda Rose Park (13)	161
Christopher Harris (12)	162
Stella McNeill (12)	163
Alfie Young (13)	164
Erin Richards (12)	165
Louie Maddern (11)	166
Sophie Perryman (11)	167
Zoe Bodfish (12)	168
Isla Harvey (12)	169
Kara Clarke (12)	170
Iona Moran (13)	171
Zac H Humphreys (12)	172
Jacob Parr (11)	173

Evie Hepworth (13)	174
Pip Richards (11)	175
Elowyn Floyd-Norris (11)	176
Jake Kingsley-Heath (11)	177
Ruby Tuesday Laura Bullock (12)	178
Hope Smith (12)	179
Natalie Mitchell (11)	180
Poppy Miller (11)	181
Piran Spackman (12)	182
Isla Clode (11)	183
Jack Oscar Ellis (12)	184
Rowan Goostrey (11)	185
Hettie Brown (12)	186
Sam Hitchens (13)	187
Henry Myles (12)	188
Ileana Eleni Karsa (11)	189
Ava Mallett (12)	190
Jacob Allen (12)	191
Jacob Taylor-McHale (12)	192
Ysabelle Iles (12)	193
Ollie Budge (11)	194
Elik Olivia Poole (12)	195
Erin Ward (13)	196
Jodie Wyatt (11)	197
Ruby-June Grunberger-Miles (12)	198

West Buckland School, West Buckland

Tommy Burrows (12)	199
Daisy Whelan (11)	200
Isaac Spear (12)	201
Isabella Watts (13)	202
Vincent Burton (12)	203

THE STORIES

Lights Out!

The abyss. The virtual competition to win blissful life. Sirens sound and the lights cease. I'm running, but I can't hold on for much longer. The blood-curdling screams of my opponents sicken me as the beast that roams silences them. They're dropping like flies. I'm terrified. I'm blind and can't tell where it's coming from. But I have my little friend, my titanium 32-inch blade with a leather hilt. I firmly stand my ground, squeezing my sword. Suddenly, the monster growls lowly behind me. My blade is struck from my hand. I'm pushed back, the fear gripping my body...

Renée Henry (13)
Edgbaston High School For Girls, Edgbaston

Missing

I couldn't find her, I looked everywhere: the garden, pillows and I even snooped around in the next-door neighbour's garden. I could hear Mother slowly but loudly trotting down the stairs. She asked me in a worried tone, "Where is she?" I replied, "Umm, we are playing hide-and-seek." (Part of it was true, although she didn't want to be found.) After she brought what I said, I immediately thought to myself it was game over! When I dropped to the ground, I saw my beloved, fluffy, cute and pale white rabbit! Thankfully, the hunt was over!

Hannaya Sajid (12)
Edgbaston High School For Girls, Edgbaston

The Greatest Gift

The hunt was on! There was a competitive race to find out who could buy the greatest gift for the infamous Ms Ajmal on her birthday. Although no one had a clue what to get, everyone was eager to win the marvellous, benevolent Ms Ajmal's approval and consequently, be crowned her favourite! We all scoured every inch of every shop, store or stall in town. Haste filled the air, however I had a secret treasure of my own. My present was a mahogany cut-out of her favourite saying: "Read, Relaxation, Radio 4!" But the question was, would it be enough?

Siena Henry (13)
Edgbaston High School For Girls, Edgbaston

The Prey

I ran at full speed across the forest floor. My snowy white pelt was glistening with sweat. I couldn't go on for much longer... My eyes were darting everywhere, desperately looking for an exit. The softskins were fast approaching, their death stick in hand. *Bang!* I heard the cutting of the death ball as it whizzed past me. I dodged another one just in time. My snout began to pick up the scent of my worst fear... Fire! I looked back to see the softskins igniting trees with tongues of flame. They were burning down the forest, my dear home...

Carmen Lucia Sánchez Diamente (12)
Edgbaston High School For Girls, Edgbaston

Survive

I couldn't run for much longer as I gasped for air, entering the cottage to hide from what killed my parents.

The thick stench of corpses was all around me. Scared and trembling with fear, I looked for a place to hide until this nightmare ended. I ran down to the cellar and climbed into a cupboard. I started crying, tears rolled down my cheeks. These hideous aliens were hunting everyone everywhere. No one would be safe.

Suddenly, the door opened. They had found me. What was I to do? Where would I go? Would I survive this alien invasion?

Jasmine Kalirai (11)
Edgbaston High School For Girls, Edgbaston

The Criminal

I just stole jewellery. I did it for a good reason, although I'm seen as a criminal. I'm running through the streets, leaping over cars and climbing above buildings. My heart is beating as fast as a bullet train. My hair is in a triangle of knots and my face is covered in dirt. My legs are in grief from the sprinting and the weight of the jewellery. I suddenly collapse, everywhere goes black...
I've now woken up and smell a manky medicine smell. I see policemen surround me. They've caught me. I've lost the people I love.

Cassy Molokwu (13)
Edgbaston High School For Girls, Edgbaston

The Big Ones

I can't run for much longer. My legs are failing me. The Big Ones are coming. I have twenty-four hours to recieve 'it' and save humanity. A piercing shriek is heard. They are close. Everyone I loved, gone; taken by the Big Ones. I will find my vengeance. Blindly racing through the maze of rubble, I attempt to reach the centre. Dead end. No... it can't be over yet. I still have time. *Hurry up,* I tell myself. A bright light is ahead of me. I've found it. All of a sudden, darkness closes around 'it'. Please, no! Destroyed hope...

Jannah Hussain (12)
Edgbaston High School For Girls, Edgbaston

Reindeer

The light shone on my gun, it glared back into my eyes. The metal felt heavy and unnatural. The snow crunched behind me. I spun silently and stared at the animal, its ears twitched and it galloped away. My legs were moving before I told them to. Snow splashed into my boots and froze my toes. The reindeer ran fast, but I was faster. I fingered the trigger and the antlered creature fell, blood flowing red into the crisp snow. I walked into the open and shivered from the harsh cold. I knelt down and dragged the robotic creature out.

Isobel Hemming (14)
Edgbaston High School For Girls, Edgbaston

The Chase

I felt uneasy; I could sense someone staring at me from every direction. Was I being... hunted? I couldn't run for much longer. My heart was beating so fast that I felt it could pop out of my chest any minute now. My whole body felt tense. Would they catch me? My legs couldn't bear the pain from running for so long. The wolves looked like they were full of energy and ready to pounce. I was their prey. I couldn't stop thinking about whether I would make this out alive. What was going to happen? Would I make it?

Olivia Casey (12)
Edgbaston High School For Girls, Edgbaston

Searching

It was time. The team got changed into their disguise. I was screaming on the inside! I wore my mask, we were prepared. As we weren't allowed to say our real names, we were all named after colours. I was pink, the others were green, yellow, purple and blue. Blue hacked the security in the theme park so that Yellow and I could get through slowly. I placed my bag on the security check-in. I made it through. We came for the president's daughter as she would make everything in our plan work. The search for her had begun...

Zara Khalid (11)
Edgbaston High School For Girls, Edgbaston

On The Run

The sirens blasted, I had to leave. One by one, we literally ran for our lives. Slowly, people began to get caught. I was one of the lucky ones who made it out alive and not injured. That day has scarred me for life. I'll tell you what happened...

One of my guards were cleaning my room, so I 'slipped' and pressed the emergency release button. Suddenly, everyone was out and I didn't know what to do. *Knock! Knock! Knock!* Shivering, I walked over. Two police officers were there. I know these people...

Louise Krone (11)
Edgbaston High School For Girls, Edgbaston

The Perfect Christmas Present

It was early morning. Let's get shopping! I need to buy the perfect Christmas present for Lucy. Surely it can't be that hard?

It was slowly becoming dark and I still haven't found a present. I walked through every single aisle, touching everything in my sight, yet I still couldn't find a present. Why was this taking so long? That was when I spotted it, the perfect present: a notebook. I was going to leave, but that's when I noticed the doors had closed! How was I going to get out?

Samreen Hussain (11)
Edgbaston High School For Girls, Edgbaston

The Box

It was like a game of hide-and-seek. I was running for my life. All I was doing was taking back something I'd lost the other day, then the sirens began. They had alerted a full police chase. They thought I was a criminal; I was the prey and they were the predator. I wouldn't have been surprised if they had got the army involved. It was one of the most precious items. They acted as if there was a natural disaster going on across the globe. I was very frightened of what was going to happen next...

Daisy Edmonds (11)
Edgbaston High School For Girls, Edgbaston

Venom

I will find it. I will hunt it down like the venom it is. Each step leaves a fresh, crisp footprint in the snow. It is as if I'm the only soul to have ever walked here, yet the tracks of the stray panther prove otherwise. I find her sleeping on a patch of grass that wasn't covered in the white, powdery snow. I stare. It's been years since I last saw anything as ferocious as she is. I watch, my breaths silent. After a while, I take hold of my bow, snatch on the arrow, aim... and shoot... She's dead.

Amelie Moylan (13)
Edgbaston High School For Girls, Edgbaston

Stew

My tough orange skin is buried under a mass of dry soil. The farmer lets me grow but I feel my time to see the sky is soon. He tells me to grow because stopping is painful. To be cooked, boiled or worse... chopped to death! Oh no. The shovel goes in and pulls out my body buried within. I then feel the cold metal touch my tough orange skin. My roots cut off, the water let out, I'll never be the same. I'll soon be in a boiling-hot stew being eaten by you!
I'm a dead orange carrot.

Emmie McLaughlan (13)
Edgbaston High School For Girls, Edgbaston

Lost In Nowhere

I couldn't run for much longer. My legs were shaking like I was being electrocuted. The echoes of the policeman's voice was drilling into my head. As I was sprinting round trees and bends, I could hear the crackling of leaves under the policeman's feet. He was getting close! Then, suddenly, I felt a grab from my hood and fell backwards. A bucket of dread and horror poured over me. I blacked out! As my eyes reopened, I looked around and all I could see was a white room. Where was I?

Isabel Curry (13)
Edgbaston High School For Girls, Edgbaston

Run Away To A Better Place

The air was nice here. Fresh. Different. I know that they will probably come for me eventually. I don't care. I like it here. I would like to enjoy my time. It smells of rain here. I had never really liked the smell before. Now, I find it beautiful. It never smelled like this back home.

Home. I am not too sure I ever had one. I wish to know what it feels like, though.

The leaves sway calmly in the breeze. They seem so at ease. I wish to be like that. I think I will like being here.

Manisha Ark (13)
Edgbaston High School For Girls, Edgbaston

Trapped

They're coming! I need to hide fast. Where will I go? I'm trapped. They're everywhere, they're circling the whole city, just to find me. I'm dead. What should I do? Give up or hide? Hide forever underground? Where am I supposed to get my food? I'm going to die out here. They're going to find me. I need to go, now! I can hear the heavy footsteps approaching me. They're coming from both sides... I'm trapped!

Aamnah Aqdis (13)
Edgbaston High School For Girls, Edgbaston

They Were Coming

What could I do? They were coming.
I knew there was no point, but I still ran. I ran until my chest heaved and my legs buckled, but I still didn't stop. They were closing in on me and I knew it. I sent a silent prayer to anyone who would listen, and tried to blend into the shadows. I couldn't tell if it was the cold or the sheer fear of being found that made me shiver.
What could I do? They were coming.

Martha Abbott (11)
Edgbaston High School For Girls, Edgbaston

Guns, Dogs, Silence

I'm running for my life. The pounding of footsteps are getting forever closer. Dogs barking. Dozens of guns aiming; I am the target. With every step, they are gaining on me. The blare of the gunshots echo around the canyon. I can see the canyon narrowing ahead of me, imprisoning me. The sirens are drawing in.
Then silence...

Lucy Abbott (13)
Edgbaston High School For Girls, Edgbaston

Hide-And-Seek

A scream floated daintily across the air, eventually becoming ensnared in Mark's mind. Another one down. He waited for an instant, savouring the scrap of silence that was awarded to him, before the footsteps continued, their gentle yet relentless plodding echoing through the halls, pounding faster, stronger... She was drawing near. She was going to find him, whether he was ready or not. She was a snake, traversing through the tangles of earth, remaining near silent; if you discredit those footsteps that neevr seemed to increase in volume. They were just like their own presence and they were hunting him...

Libby Ogden (13)
High Tunstall College Of Science, West Park

Falling Dreams

Falling. A nightmarish poltergeist assailing the band of youths. *Is it a dream?* I convey to suggest, as I catechize my thesis. Dreaming? Possibly. Staring at the galactic yonder, and through it... Heaven? Spacing out, a common factor I always find myself doing; the revenant hastening towards me. A putrid smell. Sickening me. As if I had to oblige to be sick.

It started as a blur, fading to pitch-black. Practically hitting the rigid terrain, I spotted topaz fur gleaming beneath the heavens above, giving spotlight to the common fox, scampering along with its youths. Then I woke...

Johnny McIntyre (11)
High Tunstall College Of Science, West Park

Scartoxin

A parasite... A virus that lurked. I can't run, or I'll be caught. 'Scartoxin'. An antibiotic gone wrong killed its own creators. Apparently, it looks like water. Only seen by the infected. I'm the only one left. I have to defeat it... I have to! I wonder if there are any other survivors. *Crash!* I turned the corner of Cartway Street to see... nothing? It was just a blank canvas of metal and rust. Until I felt like I was suddenly drowning, even though I was miles away from a freshwater source. Eventually, my eyes opened to see water.
Goodbye.

Ana-Lee Malone (12)
High Tunstall College Of Science, West Park

My Abscond From Penitentiary

I had to run. Go. Leave. The spotlights blazed down to the ground, circling me. Sirens wailed like a newborn baby, making me tremble with fear. Anxiety swarmed me. My escape from prison was easy; it was now time for the manhunt. Nerves acted as a blanket for my quivering body. Twenty-eight miles in less than an hour to reach the airport. It was my only plane to freedom. Was it possible?
The police followed my every move, they were on my back. My risky abscond from penitentiary will change my life. If I make it.

Hollie Niamh Mudd (14)
High Tunstall College Of Science, West Park

Watching...

Shadows watching... Seekers seeking... The people are watching, following our every move. No one believes me, of course, but I see. I can see them through the walls. The illusions of mirrors. I just have to sit here and wait. I might sound crazy, but you will see when we are hiding from them. You will see!
- 1987 - Insane Asylum.

Charlie Ray Turner (12)
High Tunstall College Of Science, West Park

Hunted Love

The door slammed. Once again, just left here with my contagious thoughts. Reaching out for the handle, deja vu struck me. Reciting the words, "A break would be healthy," my heart screamed. My veins ran cold. Regretting my every decision. Painfully persued. Crying to the devil. Round the raging wheels went with all my dignity attached. The race was on. Wiping off my shoes, my inner cheetah came out. Banging the window, he smirked. It was over. A trail of tyre marks was all that was left. Eyes swimming in tears, seeing twenty years of love, the hunt was over.

Holly Aston (15)
Madeley Academy, Madeley

The Other Side

Panic. Panting like a dog. Realisation flickered inside whilst a low growl engulfed us all in terror. Pointy ears shot up to the night-time sky; piercing eyes threw daggers into my own. Collapsing. Coughing. Choking for breath to ask: is it really worth it anymore? Fiery lactic acid ferociously bubbled in my legs as knives of pain stabbed each and every muscle inside my fatigued body. Pain. Sickness. DIzziness. Time was running out for everyone I ever knew and loved. We sprinted like escaped bulls because, on the other side, sweet, sweet victory excited our senses...

Chloe de Boer (15)
Madeley Academy, Madeley

Final Masterpiece

The crimson liquid, now cold, trailed down my arm. A shiver went down my spine as I dirtied the knife held tightly in my fist. A puddle growing round his motionless body, I stared down at my newly created masterpiece, feeling no remorse for what I had done. Cautiously, I slid the curtain slightly to the side, allowing a shallow bit of light to pour through. Crowds of vivid colours were gathered outside, stopped by glowing yellow tape. A loud crash could be heard before quiet taps echoed through the hallway. Now it was time. They would never get me...

Faith Rubenis (15)
Madeley Academy, Madeley

The Pursuit

I couldn't run for much longer. Led by a ghost and clammy with anxiety, I bolted through the streets. A labyrinth of houses made it harder to navigate my way. My chest tightened, making my breath lessened, however, my pulse heightened. I needed to rest; they weren't close anyway. I snuck round a corner and collapsed behind a bin. The concrete was harshly cold, but it was soothing to my aching limbs. I unfastened my bag and savoured my final drop of water, letting it roll on my tongue. Hyperventilating, I rested my eyes. I couldn't run for much longer...

Olivia Merrills (14)
Madeley Academy, Madeley

Smile At The Demons In The Mirror

It's not safe now they know. Every moment of freedom I remember experiencing is a new form of torture now. When you are the hunter, there's no escape. They control the nightmares, the agonisingly blissful nightmares. The alcohol subdues them, only for an hour, and drugs don't work, they make him stronger; more freedom, less pain, gone for longer. When he comes back, each time he stays longer. All I can do is sit and ponder my sweet predicament. I crave it. I don't want it, I need it. I can't help but long for it. Crave the hunt.

Poppy Walpole (14)
Madeley Academy, Madeley

For Now...

My heart was pounding in my chest. My feet were as sore as if I'd been walking on hot coals. My body yearned for rest and to take a break from my shallow breathing and thudding footsteps. "I was away though," I kept telling myself. The cold sweats, throbbing muscles, pounding head and cuts and bruises were all worthwhile for what I had achieved. I was desperate for a sighting of a familiar face; someone to hold me and reassure me that the endless pain I'd endured would be no more. I had finally escaped my torturer. For now...

Faye Atterbury (15)
Madeley Academy, Madeley

I Can't Get Away

They're onto me. I keep running and there they are, always following. It's like I can't get away from them. I go into a shop, there they are. I turn a corner and there's always someone there.

Wind was blowing my hair everywhere, my vision blurred. It's like running away from a living nightmare. It's as terrifying as a monstrous, bloodthirsty clown. There was the crash of bins and the squeal of cats. I could hear the screech of tyres as the thudding of feet hurtled in my direction. I couldn't get away! I can't go on much longer! Help...

Tyler Sznober (15)
Madeley Academy, Madeley

The Chase

They were close. The people who hated me. The ones who didn't want me around. The ones who don't understand what's happening. The sirens wailed. I couldn't run for much longer. I had no energy left within me to power on. I had to hide somewhere. This never-ending battle between a poor, lonely young boy and the demons of the world carried on through the dark lanes of the black city. I was so close to freedom. So close. I nearly had everything I needed. Everything I *will* need. I won't ever return.
We weren't close enough...

Ben Stevens (14)
Madeley Academy, Madeley

Run!

We had to leave. Now! The Origami Killer had been killing for years. He was after everyone. He kills and leaves an origami boat there. Now he was after me and my friends. We could hear thumps behind us, he was chasing us! We instantly got to the roof and locked the door with a broom. There was no escape from him. I looked at my friends. "We have to jump."

Holly replied, "Are you mad? That's a 100-foot drop. If we miss we are done, dead."

I looked at them then jumped. They all followed. *Boom! Crack!* "The door."

Amelia Ward (14)
Madeley Academy, Madeley

The Hedgeman Hunted

The Hedgeman is a hedgehog-cross-human. We have searched for years. Finally, we have found him. We were in pursuit to catch him and extract his multipurpose DNA. Then we can make use of his species.

"Come in, come in, he's behind the bush. Get him!"

We were chasing him, we almost got him.

"Pin it down!"

"Okay, we got him."

"Take his DNA. Let's go! Take it back to the facility!"

Have you ever seen the Hedgeman before? I just got info that there is a female Hedgeman. This is a new adventure!

Thomas Harris (13)

Madeley Academy, Madeley

One Shot!

Too close, too tense, too far away. Six hours, that's all; it's clinging to me like a parasite. Thought after thought in my head of... him! He is a snowstorm, cold inside. Asking me to kill my best friend with one shot. I am not capable of this; he is basically my brother! But if I don't, I will be the one hunted...
One shot. Come on, shouldn't hurt that bad. Straight through the skull. Blood everywhere, no evidence to rely on. Brains all over the place. The job is done but this time it went way too far.

Aidan Willis
Madeley Academy, Madeley

Hunted!

Stumbling straight to the floor, I had to get up. If not he, *they* would get me. The Gorgon's green eyes were burning. The heat began to consume my sweaty skin. I was being hunted brutally. Guns were being fired and trees were collapsing. The madness would never end until I did. Out from the madness, he approached, gun in hand, heavily armed. Turning to the sight of fire, I ran and never looked back. Burning filled my sense of smell. Out from the mist he came. With one quick shot, I was on one last thread...

James Llewellyn (15)
Madeley Academy, Madeley

The Iconic Pursuit

The sirens were wailing as Tommy and Taylor ran from the police because they robbed the local shop and stole the money from the bank. The sirens wailed as they got closer and closer. They had a gun each and bombs, but then someone came and got them and they got in the car. But the police got the tyres let down so they decided to bail on foot and did parkour to get away from the police. They couldn't because the police had the exits blocked off. Tommy and Taylor couldn't run for much longer so they gave up.

Harry Clements-Brown (13)

Madeley Academy, Madeley

The Night I Got Caught

The sirens wailed while I was running for my life. I knew what I did was wrong, but it wasn't my fault; they attacked me first. So I used self-defence, but that turned into murder. I was just wanting to have a nice night out, but it got too out of hand. I got drunk and someone tried hurting me, so I used self-defence for myself. People saw, so if I get caught I'm stuck in prison, like a mouse in a trap! They were full of ferocity. Oh no, they've found me...
Goodbye, everyone!

Ellie-Mae Hodgkiss (13)
Madeley Academy, Madeley

Hunted!

We were so close! They must be here somewhere. It was so intricate, it was perpertual. You could see two sides of the twenty-four hours. Dark, misty nights with the flowers dancing in the wind, then big cars in the city, horns beeping and sirens wailing, and the sound of someone's voice saying, "You've been hunted!" It was so complex, finding them running through the prickly, precisely pointed holly and getting stung by nasty nettles. The people being hunted jumped on beautiful, brown, chocolate-like boats, zooming through the elegant waves. The smart people hunting them jumped for joy!

Amy Call (11)
Prenton High School For Girls, Rock Ferry

The Run For Life

Rapidly, I ran down the ancient cobbled streets of Italy, my heels clicking on the ice-cold floor with my every move. I turned around, a dark black shadow appeared on the cracked walls of a gloomy alleyway. It moved. A tall ghoulish figure who had lifeless eyes started chasing me like a lion trying to catch its prey. He had a sharp metallic blade. He was ready to pounce. I tried to find a way out. There was no hope. There was nothing to do, nothing to think. Stranded on the ancient street, all alone, how could I escape?

Fatima Rahman (12)

Prenton High School For Girls, Rock Ferry

The Hunted

It was a cold winter's night. I was stuck in the woods. My fur was sticking up on my skin and I could hear other wolves howling. That's when I heard it. The crumpling of the winter leaves, footsteps getting closer and closer. It was the same cold-hearted man coming to get me! His gun was always running out after he shot birds. It was impossible to escape. Now I was the hunted. He was just behind a tree, until another wolf jumped out and attacked him. Now I am not the hunted anymore, I am completely kill-free!

Alissa Wright (11)
Prenton High School For Girls, Rock Ferry

The Night Of The Living Dead...

There I was, running for my life...

That day, he had taken the one thing we were warned about! Shaking, I hid behind my grandfather's gravestone. His grimy claws scraped across the stones like they were on a blackboard. I tried digging into the ground to hide, but all of a sudden, a bony mouldy hand gripped my foot. I screamed! Men were crawling from the ground! Without a doubt, I ran but then I blacked out. I woke up to see him, the one who murdered them. I lay in my own blood. This was how I ended.

Skye Penlington (12)

Prenton High School For Girls, Rock Ferry

Almost Gone!

I woke up, I realised I only had nineteen hours until I wasn't anything anymore. I rushed downstairs and darted out of the door. When I got to the bus stop, there was a man following me, so I ran towards the forest and I heard a gunshot. The man was right behind me. He was after me, he was hunting me. I wondered why, but I turned to him and he was confused. I told him that it wasn't nice and he would have an unhappy life if he did this.
So he stopped and we both smiled.

Lucy Barnett (11)
Prenton High School For Girls, Rock Ferry

A Hunter's Story

I am out of breath. I need to find some place to hide. I should have listened to my wife; she told me my job was dangerous. Shh; everything is quiet, he must have given up. I can finally go home and recieve a kiss from my love. I didn't catch the bear, so that means more hate from my boss, but at least I am alive. I can finally tell my kids my story. It will mean the world to me if my kids grow up to be hunters because of my story. It really would mean the world.

Georgia Linton (11)
Prenton High School For Girls, Rock Ferry

It's Not Safe

"Quick! It's not safe, they know."
"Jackie, we have to leave before we're taken."
"Taken where?"
"You know where, Billy."
Bang!
"They're here, Billy. Run!"
"Get the girl, dispose of Billy."
Pow!
"B-Billy! N-no! Get off me, get away!"
"We know what you've done, Jackie..."
My stomach fell to the floor. As she screamed, the walls inside that room held secrets no one would ever uncover. Jackie O'brian vanished. Where did she go? they ask. Well, that's one secret I'll never tell! Will you?

Mia Barnett (14)
Prince Henry's High School, Evesham

Something Was Watching ...

Crisp, fragile leaves crunched underfoot. The smell of fresh pine lingered in a dense, hot haze. In the distance, buried in a thick carpet of leaves, something rustled. Sunlight hit the trees, dispersing gold rays upon the ground. Beneath the thick cluster of delicate, parched vegetation: a mouse. Brown, velvety and innocent, slowly beginning to move. Something was watching. Something was glaring. Something was wanting. Something wanted to kill. Something would kill. But the sleek, silky, wire-like whiskers had not sensed the smell of death, nor any smell of danger! Claws dug, adrenaline rushed, eyes widened. Silence.

Robyn Yates (13)
Prince Henry's High School, Evesham

Hunted

To hunt or be hunted. The rules, the only rules. The perpetual, frantic beating of my heaving chest. Anxiety and paranoia writhe within the barren land of little flesh, blood congealing on lifeless spirits, but I was passive as I was obsessed with my eventual goal. Abruptly, an unknown figure grasped at my throat. Unfazed, I did the deadly deed. It collapsed, it was dead. I proceeded with my task. Shaken. Tormented. Regretful of my 'choice'? No. I did my duty. *Crunch.* I started hearing noises. Were they here? I sped up my sprint. I turned and I was captured...

Isabel Jane Fairchild (15) & Stella Lewis-Painter (14)
Prince Henry's High School, Evesham

The Mask

The laughter of the fairground cackled in my ears, the wind's bitter glance turning bright lights into a messy patchwork high above. Silver clouds grew from my mouth as I breathed silently into the night. I watched as children ran happily, their laughter becoming distorted, growls under the eerie fairground sang. A tsunami of guilt flooded over me like a whisper almost silent in my ear. My hands grasped hard around it behind my back, my fingertips digging hard into my palms. Again, I looked at the happiness of the fairground, but it was only a mascarade hiding truth beneath...

Megan Bearcroft (14)
Prince Henry's High School, Evesham

The Purge

I still have nightmares about it. The Purge. That one day. It has consumed my every thought. Leaving my mind paralysed and me alone. The day was cold. The day was almost like a claw machine, picking and choosing who lives, who dies. He stood next to me, sweat dripping. My mind was racing like a predator coming for its prey. He looked me in the eyes, terror snapping away. The speaker announced the commencing. Life won't be the same. Laying there, people falling down, never seen, never heard. Like him. Terror leaving in handcuffs. Leaving me imprisoned. I'm stranded...

Ruby McLennan (13)
Prince Henry's High School, Evesham

Paranoia

They're trying to get me. I've done something terrible. They're looking for me. I sprint through an overgrown forest path, adrenaline pumping round my body, sweat streaming down my tear-soaked face, muscles aching. I know they're behind me, screams of my name ring through my ears. Trees tower over me, trapping me, working with the night to impair my vision. A dozen silhouettes appear, taunting me, closing in on me. My screams land on deaf ears as they surround me. I launch my fist at an evil grin, but meet nothing. They're gone, my mind banishing my paranoid thoughts.

Daniel Spencer (14)
Prince Henry's High School, Evesham

Twenty Dead Homeless Begging For My Well-Earned Money

I had twenty-four hours and the sirens wailed in the background. I couldn't run for much longer. The cop cars were two feet behind me. I still have nightmares about it coming and coming after me for twenty-four days. I'm regretting what I've done. Wanna know what I've done? Well, are you ready? I murdered twenty homeless people and now the police have been after me for twelve years. Do I regret it? No I don't! Because these homeless deserved it, begging for my well-earned money! Well, they're not having it today, not on my watch. No way.

Connor Nash (13)
Prince Henry's High School, Evesham

California Max

He ran through the undergrowth, knowing that he was in trouble. Just a few minutes ago, he had escaped from the infamous California maximum security prison, known to the locals as California Max. In the distance, he could hear the whirr of a helicopter and suddenly, like a monster from the deep, the monster emerged from amongst the trees, threatening to end his life. He spotted the sniper in the boy of the helicopter and realised that now the odds of surviving and dropped down massively. To his dismay, he knew that the fight was over. He accepted his death...

Dominic Hampshire (13)
Prince Henry's High School, Evesham

The Thing

I had to keep running. I wasn't going to be beaten. No way. If I was going to keep my life, I had to keep running. It didn't help that the streets were crowded with them, but I knew where the main groups patrolled. One of the first rules of surviving the apocalypse was: 'If they can't see you, they can't shoot you.' Unfortunately, I'd forgotten that one. That's how I ended up here, running from a bunch of teens with guns down a random avenue in Hollywood. That's where my memory blacks out because I'm dead. Forgot that.

James Alexander Douglas Atkins (14)
Prince Henry's High School, Evesham

Hunted

The officer's lantern flickered in the hallway. The floorboards creaked beneath his feet as he heard screaming from the hallway. His lantern burnt out as he felt something at his feet. He looked down and, to his horror, there was a body stabbed and cut beyond recognition. As the officer looked around in horror, he saw nothing but darkness. He heard a faint sound coming from the dark silhouette of a wardrobe. He crept over to it, he looked inside and saw two piercing red eyes staring at him. But something was wrong...
It was his own reflection.

Alex Impey (15)
Prince Henry's High School, Evesham

The Silhouette

I couldn't run much longer. I was sprinting through the dark, deep forest when I saw a black silhouette that was just standing there. It started to slowly follow me. I ran faster and faster. I looked around and it was there, a strange depressing creature. It tried to grab me, I felt so anxious, I didn't know what I was going to do. I darted towards the local town, I couldn't see anything. There were things getting thrown at me with force. The creature had a dangerous speed. I turned around and faced the weird, spooky, lifeless creature...

Euan James Aspey (14)
Prince Henry's High School, Evesham

The Escape

I had twenty-four hours. The soldiers would not stop searching. The dogs would not stop tracking. There was nowhere to go. As I watched the bright light shine off one leaf to the next, I finally found the underground bunker I've been searching for, for hours. Only there's one problem; I need to find the key. It's on one of the trees. The problem is they're all covered in thick green moss. I started searching but the guards were so close now and I didn't know whether I was going to get in. But then I finally saw something shiny...

Amber Johns (14)
Prince Henry's High School, Evesham

Through The Fields

Dark, cold, foggy. That's what a 'normal' winter night contains. Out in the fields, after running away from home, sirens sounded in the distance, trying to find me. They were stalking me like a lion hunting its prey. Down, into the boggy banks of the stream that flowed. To the sparkly icy field. *Crunch!* I heard leaves behind me crackle as something approached. I turned around and I could see flashlights through the trees. I froze. I didn't know what to do. I stood still, frozen with fear. Were they going to catch me or would I get away?

Olivia Ormsby (13)
Prince Henry's High School, Evesham

The Search

It was day one of the search. We were walking through the woods silently to reach our destination, when a man stepped out from behind the tree.

"Where are you going?"

"We're looking for our puppy, his name's Pom. I lost him a few weeks ago."

"Carry on then," he replied.

We thought nothing of it and carried on. I reached out my hand to knock on a door when the man jumped out again! As quick as a flash, we ran as fast as we could. But my baby brother... he was gone! We never saw him again...

Lily-Grace Riley (14)
Prince Henry's High School, Evesham

The Final Battle

Twenty-four hours ago it all started...

Scanning my surroundings, I spotted him. This is what I had been waiting for. My life depended on this. Lining up my shot, my teeth chattered with nerves. I pulled the trigger. It missed! Then, lining up another shot, I saw him aiming right at me. Swiftly ducking, I saw my life flash before my eyes. A bullet went flying past my head. Returning fire, I got a hit. Pushing towards him, I hit him again. This time, the finishing shot. I screeched excitedly.

I won the Nerf battle. The cup was mine!

Daniel Wilde (14)
Prince Henry's High School, Evesham

The Escape

Many years we've been plotting to escape this place. Every day, we planned and practised every detail... I remember it was a Tuesday. All of us put into endless lines. One by one, they installed a chip in our palms. I was terrified. I got caught up in a crime scene. They put me and twenty others into a van, with loads of intimidating officers. I could feel the frosty air coming in through the window. Outside, the prison loomed above us: a grey wall surrounded by razor wire. It's been six years, I will reclaim what they stole...

Dylan James Ferris (13)
Prince Henry's High School, Evesham

The Run

I still have nightmares about it... the sirens flickering! We rushed into the horror. Hours ago, John invited us to his humongous maze. He was hesitant of asking us. Still, we entered anyway, wary of all the surroundings. The last time people entered, they never came out...

Hours before being found, we were panting, sprinting away. He found us, he caught us, I was found. I nearly won the game of hide-and-seek. They breached the gate. What happened still has never been mentioned. What happened still haunts me like a tattoo on my brain!

Finton Jay Kilbey (13)
Prince Henry's High School, Evesham

It

I tripped, blood streaked from my face and my pulse was stuttering. The lab was grief-stricken. Sparks of fire sprayed up, shards of glass were scattered all over the floor. There was nowhere for me to hide. Nowhere. Screeches echoed through the soulless halls. I knew it couldn't have been far; I needed to hide. The flickering lights flashed in the dim room. I heard the thing getting nearer. Where could I go? My eyes twitched towards a light cupboard. I limped over and squished my body in and slammed the door. I heard it breathe...

Harry Hughes (13)
Prince Henry's High School, Evesham

Hit And Run!

I was not ready for the unexpected. I was shaking, cold and blood was surrounding me everywhere I looked. I started to panic and my heart was racing out of my chest. I had no idea what to do until a random person approached me. The person proceeded to call emergency services while I was screeching in pain! Tears were rolling down my face and I was wondering to myself, *why is it always me?* A few minutes later, the person started to put pressure on my wound so less blood would pour out my body...
Wrong place, wrong time.

Alexa Hewitt (13)
Prince Henry's High School, Evesham

Surrounded

They were after me. I couldn't run for much longer. I've been running for hours, trying to escape them. Thunder cracked above me. Crisp leaves crunched under my feet. The cold air whipped my face as I forced my aching legs to carry on running. I wouldn't let them catch me, no. Not after last time. I still have the marks from the beating. Droplets of rain ran off the branches like blood. All of a sudden, a dark, tall figure blocked my path. I swung my head round, everywhere I looked there were people. I was surrounded...

Emily Drake (13)
Prince Henry's High School, Evesham

Hunted

The searing rays of blistering sun shone down on the endless dunes like relentless cold in the Arctic. I was beginning to stumble as the lifeless sandy desert that stretched far beyond the horizon had taken its toll on my legs. Abruptly, I fell onto my knees. I quickly took off my weighty backpack and pulled out the bottle, which was now empty. I tried to force the last little drop of water out of the bottle, but with limited success. Dehydrated, I lay there witnessing the Jeep that was after me roll over the hill. I was finished.

Matty Watton
Prince Henry's High School, Evesham

Don't Look Right...

I'm the shadow you see from the corner of your eye. Or more accurately, five years and three months ago. I keep track of you. I keep track of everyone. Remember that horror movie? I was there. Stood in the corner of the room. Watching... You saw me once. You looked to your left. I do that sometimes. To distract you from what's on your right... Because if you had seen it, it would have killed you. The breathing you sometimes hear at night. It's never stood on your left... Can you hear it? Don't. Look. Right.

Amber Davis (15)
Prince Henry's High School, Evesham

Hunted

"We have to leave. Now." Jasper's icy fingers grabbed my hand and led me to the door. "We don't have a choice, they are coming to find us, no matter what, Briar." As he spoke, I could hear the guards' footsteps coming down the corridor. Before I took another breath, we were running for our lives with the guards chasing after us. My life was flashing before my eyes. Jasper was the only thing that mattered now; I had to get him safe, even if it meant sacrificing my life. One shot fired behind me, this was my last breath...

Francesca Hayward (14)
Prince Henry's High School, Evesham

Hide-And-Seek

I still have nightmares about it; the cold night still sends chills down my spine. It was just a game of hide-and-seek. It shouldn't have gone that far. He shouldn't have come inside. He shouldn't have seen, I told him to hide in his bedroom and I would come in two minutes, but he didn't listen. Why didn't he listen? Everything was going to plan. He was supposed to be in his room. It shouldn't have happened! He was only six. It should have been me. It was *his* fault. He should have stayed outside! Now he's dead.

Sophie Webb (15)
Prince Henry's High School, Evesham

Police Chase

I couldn't catch my breath. The blue lights became more clear to see. Blood was running down my face. I'd been running for miles, not knowing where I was or where they were. I came across an open car in the street. Wasn't worth it. Then I saw a hole in a barbed-wire fence, so I knelt down and plunged my way through, making the hole a lot bigger. As I got to the other side of the fence, I could hear whispers coming from a distance, footsteps getting closer and closer, then a face that I recognised appeared...

Ruby Gould (14)
Prince Henry's High School, Evesham

Hunted

We have to leave. Now... *Crunch!* Leaves rustling in the distance. I'm hiding for my life. I was petrified. It sounded and looked like a gloomy dream. The moon was as bright as the sun with marble effects. I had twenty hours to win. I was still bawling my eyes out. This was a horror. I starved myself. I smelled petrol, I heard sirens. I ducked under the twisted tree. All I saw were bright lights with cobalt and inflamed lights jumping over me, searching for me. Then I heard a loud swoosh of air above me...

Nichola Davenhill (13)
Prince Henry's High School, Evesham

Hunted

I'm being hunted. I'm scared to look behind me. I keep getting messages from someone, sending me photos of where I've just been. I'm being hunted. I start running into places I've never seen in my life. The messages start coming through quicker, photos of me running. Pushing and bashing through people, rushing through shops, trying to get away, I find myself on a bridge, confused and shaking. Then I get a buzz from my phone. The message says 'Don't look behind you.' Do I look or not...?

Chloe Mills (15)
Prince Henry's High School, Evesham

Prison Break

My heart was beating and my leg was cut open, losing blood by the second. Dogs barking, I didn't know what to do. I decided to run out of the woods. Running down the road, shots fired rapidly behind me. At the end of the road, there were two cops. *Bang! Bang!* I shot them both. More cops started showing up. I had nowhere to go. They all had guns pointed at me. I had to stop. I couldn't do anything else.

"Get on the ground!"

I was sent back to prison. I was stuck back in that dump.

Nathan Warner (14)
Prince Henry's High School, Evesham

Hunted

Today, my life changed forever. I was being chased by the police. I had escaped from jail from previous crimes. The sirens started, I hid in a tree, my ears felt like they were about to blow off. Footsteps sounded beneath me. It was dark and gloomy and I couldn't see a thing. I was scared, so I sprinted as far away as I could, however, they found me. I dived into a strip of hay to try and hide. Flashlights flashed up and down, I couldn't see anything. Knives were being thrown, I desperately didn't want to be hit...

Bethany Pye (13)
Prince Henry's High School, Evesham

Acres

I saw him outside my window that morning, admiring the house, waiting for the sign. Unwillingly, I let him in, he looked in the rooms. So much space to live. He wanted to put in an offer, but I showed him the rest of the house, including both the indoor and outdoor pool and the stables with four ponies and the ten acres of surrounding land. I introduced him to the gardener and cleaners, they really liked him a lot. He still wanted to make an offer. He pulled out his card, his offer was £2million. It's not enough!

Grace Campbell (14)
Prince Henry's High School, Evesham

The Deceased

The hospital was a ghost town as I walked down the dimly-lit corridor. Lights flickered on and off frequently. The sound of my footsteps were drowned out by the penetrating scream. I began to run towards the destination of the scream when I came across a body laying in a dead-like state. I stopped as I examined the body. I stepped closer as a hand wrapped around my ankle! I screamed, knowing it was not going to be heard. I broke free and the deceased body rose. I soon realised I was going to be his next victim...

Brook Maiden (13)
Prince Henry's High School, Evesham

Chased

It's not safe now they know. I have to escape from this ancient, abandoned mansion before it's too late! The police are following me and I can't hide for much longer. My feet are numb and my legs are aching. I've been running for twenty-four hours now. I've been reported missing on the news and I have the whole town searching for me! I'm running out of places to hide and my energy is running low. My heart is beating rapidly. I just heard a noise from downstairs! The door just opened in front of me. I'm scared...

Poppy Risdale (13)
Prince Henry's High School, Evesham

The Demon...

I woke up, I must have fainted; good thing that humans didn't notice me. If they did, I'd be killed, cut to pieces. I still had nightmares about how they brutally murdered my family while I slipped away carefully. Screams kept ticking off in my brain, they attached to it. I got to my knees, shaking. From the corner of my eyes I saw bright, vibrant lights. I'm so done for. This is the last of me. I had no energy to run, so I didn't even want to try escaping. I froze, the cars enclosed me rapidly...
Goodbye.

Grace Stewart (13)
Prince Henry's High School, Evesham

The Unusual Children

Twenty-four hours ago, the test began. I have had several tests today. I'd been in a chamber with needles in me. Sorry, I haven't told you my name. It's Jack I was born in the Leicestershire Hospital. They have turned it into a science lab for all the special people. We all have a code, my code is 71219. This is a story about my suffering. It all started when I was a baby, I had tests and there was an unusual reading on the system. Now I have been separated from my family and my friends...

Jack Oliver Sanders (13)
Prince Henry's High School, Evesham

Last Days On Earth

I couldn't run much longer. They were coming but it was all I could do. I had twenty-four hours and the night left; the infected were coming. The sirens wailed, zombies were everywhere! They were on the hunt for more infected souls. It was like hide-and-seek but with bloodhounds. You can't hide, they can smell you. There is no one to help you. I was on my own. I still regret infecting him, but it doesn't matter now, there is nothing I can do. I miss him and now he is gone. "Goodbye."

Rhys Christopher Ayres (13)
Prince Henry's High School, Evesham

Police Chase

The siren started, I had three police cars behind, I was jumping over people's walls to get into other gardens. There was a helicopter following and circling me. I jumped into a green recycling bin and waited for the police to go past and go far enough away from me so I could run without them seeing me. I ran into the shop and robbed some drinks and some food. I took a car and started driving far away, but there was something wrong. There was a police car following me. I started to speed up. I ran away...

Matt Carter (14)
Prince Henry's High School, Evesham

My Russian Adventure

The Russians found out my secret. Three days before, my mission was to get some of the most high profile information from a secret Russian facility. I was there for two weeks... I got the info but, when I was leaving, I ran into some trouble. Running away, a Russian guard saw me, he was trained to kill. Two shots fired, two shots missed. I dropped to the ground, they cornered me. The guard was about to shoot from behind. He dropped... It was my commander! He said, "Let's get out of here."

Sam Livingstone (13)
Prince Henry's High School, Evesham

Trapped

The forest path was dull. A shrill sound pierced the sky. It was closing in on me. My heart pounded, with every beat it leapt out of my chest. My breath came out in short sharp bursts. My legs started to ache; I couldn't stop. I wouldn't stop. Panic drove me to accelerate. An eerie squeal came from the right somewhere. I came to a sudden halt; a tree had fallen on the dim pathway. No! What now? I'd come so far. I turned around quickly, it was mine now. It had fallen right into my trap...

Megan Bradley (14)
Prince Henry's High School, Evesham

The Chase

I couldn't run for much longer. My lungs shrivelled up, my legs felt like they were broken, but I couldn't stop or it would find me. As it was shifting from night to day, I slowly became more exposed. As I heard a siren, I panicked. My eyes started wandering. I saw a vending machine. My legs felt as hard as stone but moved on their own across the floor. As the police car increased in speed, I heard a horn go. As I turned around, the car slowed down. The door opened but no one was there...

Max Seadon (15)
Prince Henry's High School, Evesham

Hunted

In a place far away, a boy left the world behind and went exploring. He was determined to find out about wildlife. Now, when this boy got close to finding out about wildlife, it went wrong. He was so close to getting it once, he nearly made a breakthrough, but then failed. He was travelling one time, then a big animal rose up to then roar at the boy. Then it began to chase him through the jungle and through the ruttiest of conditions. It nearly killed him with its big paws swaying everywhere...

Jamie Beeson (14)
Prince Henry's High School, Evesham

Young Crime

I remember it clearly. It was a normal day, taking stuff from A to B, however, as I was doing what I do best, three all-black-hooded men attacked me. They took all of the stuff. I called 'Spiky', this call went on for a long time, but the main message was: "You have twenty-four hours to give me 3k cash." So I had twenty-four hours to pay up the money or my life was at risk.

The next day passed, I didn't have the money, I got chased. I couldn't run much longer. I knew it was over...

Fletcher Ford (13)

Prince Henry's High School, Evesham

Running

I was walking home from school through the forest. Every time I came close to the graveyard, my heart raced like a leopard. As soon as my foot stepped past the graveyard gate, I walked quickly. I felt someone looking at me. I looked behind me, an old man with a long beard... I went up to him and asked if he wanted help. He said, "No thank you," so I turned around cautiously and heard a scream. He was gone, out of the blue. I started running, it felt like hours. Then I heard him again...

Lilly Myler (13)
Prince Henry's High School, Evesham

Hide

I could feel my heartbeat in my throat. My feet slammed against the floor as I forced my body weight forward. My surroundings were unclear and my vision was blurred. All I knew was that I was not safe and I had to keep on moving. They knew I had something they wanted and I knew they would kill to get it back. I could hear the wheels of their cars skid against the twisty desert road. We were isolated. If I were to disappear now, no one would claim they were a witness. I had to hide now.

Ashleigh May Louth (15)

Prince Henry's High School, Evesham

Police Chase

I've made a terrible mistake. We are on the run from the police. The reason is we have robbed Home Bargains. It was me, Ben and Terry. We thought it would be funny, but it was far from it. As soon as we heard the sirens, we bolted it out. We are now in the middle of nowhere. The police are after us. There is no escape now. My legs are jelly, my breathing is messed up. I can't do this anymore. We are approaching a main road, there are police waiting. We have been well and truly caught.

Jay Merrett (14)
Prince Henry's High School, Evesham

Twenty-Four Hours Of Hide-And-Seek

I had twenty-four hours to hide. The game of hide-and-seek started. But it wasn't a normal game. If you get caught, you die! 100 seekers, 100 hiders, they have guns and knives, we have nothing. The place we hid was the size of Wales. There was a prize if you win - you stay alive. They forced you to play; we had no choice. My family were wondering where I was. There were animals in the zone and we had to fight them off with nothing. When will this end? I'm scared for my life.

William Jarvis (13)
Prince Henry's High School, Evesham

Hunted

I am in the forest when, all of a sudden, I am lost! I don't know what to do; my phone has no signal and I don't have a map. I start panicking, I have no idea what to do. If I go deeper, I might risk getting even more lost, or I could try and retrace my steps. Then suddenly, I hear leaves rustling behind me. It sounds like it's getting even closer. So I decide to run into the forest, even deeper, but *it* could result in saving my life. Now it starts coming from all angles...

Sam Spear (13)
Prince Henry's High School, Evesham

Hunted

I had thirty minutes to reach the border, otherwise I'm dead.
I jumped into the car. It was a 35-minute drive to the border.
I had to go fast to make it, but then... the bushes started to
sway fast, and animals kept hitting the car and falling over.
Then, all of a sudden, the car flipped and flew to the edge of
a cliff. I was right next to it, right next to the border. If I got
out, I would fall or die from not getting there. I decided to
jump and leap across. I just made it...

Jake Walding (13)
Prince Henry's High School, Evesham

It's Over

My legs burnt like fire; each step felt like a mile. I took a deep breath, the flicker of pain felt as if 100 bee stings dug into me! His face was tattooed in my brain. Never forgotten. I knew it was him. The trees looked down at me, their arms frantic. I collapsed like my soul shot out of my body! I dreaded to look down, but I knew it was broken. He was right in front of me, his red eyes locked onto me. The steps got closer and louder. He looked at me, I know it's over...

Joshua Neal (14)
Prince Henry's High School, Evesham

The Chase

I couldn't run for much longer. Twigs snapped under my feet as I stumbled. Thin, crisp, cold air filled my lungs and scratched my throat. Time was my enemy! Moisture on the leaves dripped like blood. The wind started to pick up and the gusts felt like a knife cutting my face. The clock was ticking; I could hear it in my head. A knot in my stomach tightened. It was now or never! The low glow of light from the moon shone down on me.
It's over, my time has come...

Carmen West (13)
Prince Henry's High School, Evesham

Running

I couldn't run for much longer, blood rushed to my face, and my lungs, deprived of air, felt as if they had been torn out of my body, then pushed back through my throat into place. I didn't know how far I had got, I felt like I had run for hours alone, afraid, unaware. My head was spinning, I could still hear the shouting voices ringing in my head in perfect chorus with the booming storm above, raining down on me. Why did I kill her? And why did I run away?

Leah Saunders (13)
Prince Henry's High School, Evesham

Hunted

It was nine o'clock and I was lying in bed when I heard some howling sounds. I went outside to go looking for where the howling sound was coming from, then... I saw a grey wolf eyeing me up. I went back home. I was unlocking my door when I saw a grey wolf sitting next to me! I jumped. I let him in and he went straight onto my sofa. Then I saw that on the floor was a pool of blood. The wolf had a massive hole through his chest. I took him straight to the vets...

Mason Rimmer (13)
Prince Henry's High School, Evesham

The Stabbing Hunter!

It is not safe now they know what I am doing to my sister. She is screaming her life away with no help. No other sound around but the howling of the wind. My parents don't know but it's getting very close to the end of life for me. Life is scary. My sister is dying slowly. I have a good feeling that I am gonna leave her. I hear sirens. I stab her and run, leaving her to bleed to death. I run for my life. I do not get as far as planned because I got caught.

Natasha Powell (13)
Prince Henry's High School, Evesham

Hunted

I was cold, freezing cold. I woke up, eyes not open yet, and I could not feel the icy bitterness on me. It was so cold, like I was in a freezer. I hope that when I opened my eyes I would be in Iceland, but there I was, lying dead still on a cold metal table. My clothes were taken and a paper-thin sheet was over me. A lady came in with some clothes and put them on the table, they were torn and muddy. I put them on and they stank. I saw a door and I ran!

Scarlett Begley (13)
Prince Henry's High School, Evesham

Police Chase

We saw a really nice pair of trainers, but they were out of our budget, so we decided to make a move and steal a pair each. When we were all ready, we legged it out of the store and all the way out of the shopping centre, towards the bus stop. But before we got there, the police found us and started chasing us. We thought we didn't have time to wait for the bus, so we just ran until we were safe and all clear of the police. Was all of this worth it?

Ben Powell (13)
Prince Henry's High School, Evesham

Hunted

I couldn't run any longer. My legs ached, my arms hurt, my heart beat like a drum and all of a sudden there it was; the wolf from the hospital. The wolf that killed all the patients. Later that day, I saw it again, so I decided to follow it. We were walking for hours. When we stopped, we were in the woods. Then we heard a scream coming from the house on the edge of the woods...

Kiera Brennan (14)
Prince Henry's High School, Evesham

Zombie Terror

We have to leave this country, zombies screaming at us, running after us. We're so tired, we can't run any longer. Our legs are throbbing. I think we've lost them! We are scared for our lives. We can't see anyone about. It is a dark, cold day. They're not here anymore. Palms sweating with fear, thinking they're behind us, let's head home now. Walking in the woods, the zombies jump out. Hair sticking up, running as fast as we can, we get home, lock all doors and just chill. I can't believe this happened. I was scared at the time!

Chelsea Terry (15)
The Meadows School, Dove Holes

Run Like Never Before

No words, just the constant thought, *run.*

"I... can't... keep... going..." She slowed to a stop. However, the constant thought of the approaching authorities kept me moving swiftly forward. They could not know. And I was the main culprit.

"Keep going... I can hear them!" I cried, the sound of roaring engines grew gradually closer until I could feel the ground shaking beneath me. "Run, run, run!" I screamed, until my voice grew hoarse.

"My... legs... ow!" said Alice, my sister.

"Come on, Alice, we have to get away!"

And after that, there was silence.

"Cut! Well done, everyone."

Phoebe Nel (12)
The Roseland Academy, Tregony

Don't Cry For Help, Else They Will Come Running

The footsteps of the kidnapper echoed across the concrete floor as he strode towards me.

"They are after us, and it's all your fault!" he growled. I tried to wriggle my hands free of the tight rope that was holding me back. In the distance, wailing sirens screamed towards our hiding place. I tried to speak, but then I remembered the tape tight over my mouth. Torchlights flashed past windows, loud voices echoed, "Show yourself!" He grabbed me and dragged me behind a cracked pillar. Footsteps moved towards us.

"Don't cry for help, else they will come running."

Erin Sylvia Gilmour (11)

The Roseland Academy, Tregony

The Monster

"Run! Run! Run! It's coming!" screamed Milo. He ran as fast as his scrawny little legs could carry him.

"What is?" Stephanie called.

"The monster!" he wailed. Stephanie screamed very loud and very clear. Milo had to cover his ears. "Hurry up!" Milo panted. "You might not make it with those chicken legs."

"Hey! That's not fair!"

Milo continued to run. 3mph, 5mph, 7mph; he couldn't run much faster as he was only five. He slowed down, tiredness spreading across his reddening face.

"Children!" shouted their mum. "Get off Grandma's treadmill!"

"Sorry, Mummy," they said in unison.

Ariane Trewinnard (12)

The Roseland Academy, Tregony

Running From Vegetable Monopoly

"Nearly there!" he panted. "Almost near London!"

He was on the run from his granny who really wanted to play 'Vegetable Monopoly', although Stanley was *not* going to play 'Vegetable Monopoly'. He was thoroughly on the run to London town. He heard a small buzzing noise approaching him like a stressed fly. Stanley turned around to see his granny on her orange mobility scooter, waving a grey wrinkly hand. It was only when she pulled up beside an out-of-breath Stanley that he noticed that the mobility scooter was playing the 'Spice Girls' on full blast.

"Vegetable Monopoly, Stanley?"

Evie Howard (11)
The Roseland Academy, Tregony

Place In The Sun

"I had twenty-four hours... twenty-four hours to find the most perfect place in the sun for my good friend here, Susan!" Jasmine Haran spoke into her microphone much too enthusiastically. The camera panned to a grinning Susan. "So, where will we be looking today?" Jasmine prompted, her lipstick seven shades too dark, shining in the sun. Susan hissed loudly into the microphone, staring into the camera. "I want a holiday home in mainland Spain today Jasmine, please." Jasmine Haran gave a forced smile.
"Alright, let's go on a house hunt then!"
The pair followed out of the camera view.

Evie-Mae Arthur (12)

The Roseland Academy, Tregony

Water After River

The mud was thick; the sky crystallized into thousands of fireflies, flickering into the anonymous abyss of the night. Rain whistled through the air, shattering elderly pebbles below, withering them to rubble. Thunder impaled the sky. Its echoes commenced like the birds that flew from the falling trees; the branches were engulfed by the inferno and ceased to exist.

A child, small for her size, was scrambling left to right, seeking some shelter. A safe spot. Mighty roars pulsated the ground. Vibrated the pebbles, making her body tremble. A scream gave way; her body fell to the floor to rest.

Ryan Marshall (14)
The Roseland Academy, Tregony

Game Dream

Running, I knew that they were close. I didn't think that it would go this far; a simple game. It had lasted for hours now. They wouldn't come back for me, so naturally, I was the only one who was found. "Aah!" I shouted, falling over a dead body rotting away in the pale moonlight. I grabbed the knife that was stuck in their chest and held it close so that I could see.
"Stop!"
They'd found me.
"You're coming with me!"
The wrong place at the wrong time... Suddenly, a shout came from downstairs.
"Come on, time for tea!"

Maisie Coombe-Gollop (11)
The Roseland Academy, Tregony

The Beast Behind Me

I couldn't breathe. The beast behind me was incredibly strong and tall. Blood drew patterns down my face, my legs black and blue, but nonetheless, I kept running. My feet beneath me were moving faster than they had ever gone. "I wish I could run the fastest on sports day, I wouldn't be here then!" I mumbled, getting distracted.
Smash! My glasses were shattered on the marble floor behind me. I longed to fall to the ground, surrounded by the debris of my glasses, breaking into tears, but I didn't. He followed me around the corridor as the bell rang...

Elena Grace Waugh (13)
The Roseland Academy, Tregony

Hide-And-Seek

"Why don't we play hide-and-seek?" asked the small girl.
"Sure, I'll hide first," the boy replied.
"One, two, three..." the girl counted. He looked around him, he ran to the bedroom, making as little noise as possible. He climbed under the bed, moving some boxes aside.
"Ready or not, here comes hunter!" came an adult's creepy, deep, ghastly, croaking voice. Heavy footsteps came into the bedroom. These weren't the feet of a small girl... A loud growling sound came from the room.
"I found you!" came a deep voice from under the bed. The boy turned around.
"Argh!"

Luke Montagu (11)
The Roseland Academy, Tregony

The Ending Of The Crops

The crops were bathing in the sun as usual, but there was one crop that stood out. He was the tallest in the field and his friends around him were nice, they were talking and chilling. They were talking about the new crop box game, Farming Simulator 59. They hated it because it's about them dying, being harvested. The one special crop was called Jimmy. Jimmy was nice. He said, "Farming Simulator is so bad."
Jimmy's friends said, "I know, showing people how to kill us!"
Then they heard the harvester.
"*Nooo!*" Jimmy said while crying...

Leo McGovern
The Roseland Academy, Tregony

Apocalypse

Life will never be the same. Everyone over eighteen was turned into a ghoul! All of this happened after the radiation planet had an overdose. Everyone under eighteen split up into different tribes. There were the Fungis, they only party. The Shepherds, they farm all day. And then there is the Sportlives, all the footballers come together and they do an annual arena fight. They select nobodies and make them fight to the death. Every tribe has their own territory. If you enter another tribe's territory, you never ever leave. The only important thing is survival. I am being hunted.

Fintan Lawler (12)
The Roseland Academy, Tregony

The Inevitable

It's coming. It's finally here. It's all our fault. The dark abyss is reclaiming our vulnerable cities, not stopping, not taking a single breath. My heart starts dancing in my chest. I watch, helpless, my feet paralysed, frozen to the ground. It is getting closer, consuming all I have ever known. It destroys everything in its path. It is invincible. The hairs on my arm stand on end like weak soldiers standing to attention, waiting for inevitable defeat. The harsh glare of the sun beams down on me, penetrating through my skin, burning me alive. The sea has finally risen.

Ellie Hancock (13)
The Roseland Academy, Tregony

Formula X

The sirens wailed, bellowing across the wildly spread abyss of darkness. Formula X was our only hope now. I grabbed the gun and made a break for the light. Something was holding me back. Someone. Oh goodness, it was one of 'them'. I gave a punch and made another break for life. "Shaun!" a figure spoke out from the black empty space. It was playing tricks with my mind. My legs started to move into the blackened atmosphere. They were moving without intention. I tried and tried, they wouldn't budge. Holding onto a pole, I had to let go!
Gone.

Harry Frederick Lutey (13)
The Roseland Academy, Tregony

The Hunters

Her mother had always kept her safe from the virus, avoiding the crazed people and the insane cults, but they couldn't hide anymore; they were being hunted. When she asked her mother why they were hunted, she only muttered something about her past. The hunters were vicious people, kept alive only by force. They aimed their guns then opened fire, but the bullets stopped, the hunters started screaming loudly as they burned. She suddenly realised why everyone seemed to want to kill her... Her mother was the virus! Her eyes burnt bright and she used her powers one last time.

Oliver John Gray (11)
The Roseland Academy, Tregony

Freedom Isn't Easy

Expressionless white walls. 5419 is my number; my only memory. Well, that and I have the deadly, infectious disease where whoever contracts it dies in thirty days. I'm on day twenty-eight. Every day is agony; the thought that one day I won't be here...

"5419, please stand," the monotone voice reads. I do so. Robust men enter in yellow suits. Here is my chance. I dart past them and run. I run till my legs are burning. I hear the sirens, I hear the shouts, but nothing is going to restrain me from my freedom.

"5419, your fun is over."

Lilah Courage (12)
The Roseland Academy, Tregony

Off The Grid

Bang! Another person dead. I ran for my life as gunfire filled the air. I was being hunted. Life was dangerous, being alive was a threat. Night was falling. *Not much further,* I thought. I stumbled and fell down, down, down. My thoughts were running in circles. I felt wet, cold. I couldn't breathe. I swam to the surface, struggling like a baby. Where was I? Maybe I was... No. I couldn't be! No! No! No! I could be obliterated. I was off the grid.
Ten years later...
Life was marvellous. I felt free and alive for once in my life.

Hannah Gulliver (11)
The Roseland Academy, Tregony

Footsteps

He dashed down the steps, desperately trying to get away from his chasers. He turned corners, sprinted down different passageways, doing anything he could to shake them off his trail. He stopped on a slim secret path. Breathing heavily, he listened for their voices or footsteps. Nothing. They had lost him. He crept along as quiet as a mouse. Silently, he walked up some stairs, hoping to be able to get inside. Suddenly, two boys appeared out of nowhere.

"Got you!" one of them said. A bell rang out in the background. "Come on," he said. "It's time for lessons."

Tremayne Richards (11)
The Roseland Academy, Tregony

The Wild Goose Chase!

I span around to find a ferocious man sprinting maliciously towards me (his eyes piercing through my soul). He wielded something vicious in his colossal hands. I couldn't run for much longer, my legs were burning and my eyes were stinging in the ice-cold wind. Exhausted, I turned around to face my opponent. "What do you want from me?"
"I'm sorry, madame," he replied, "you dropped your purse!"
Totally and utterly embarrassed, my cheeks the colour of a tomato, I turned around on my heels and began to make the shameful walk back to my house in the town!

Charlotte Gray (12)
The Roseland Academy, Tregony

The Chase

I couldn't run for much longer; my legs were aching and my feet were blistering. Panic rushed through me as the sirens became louder and louder. My heart raced, my legs trembled, my ears rang. I had to carry on. I bolted through an alleyway, footsteps now chasing behind me. Silence filled the alley. I still wasn't alone. I sprinted through the darkness, my body shivering with fear. Twisting and turning, I dodged the arms that reached out to grab me. My face became pale as I could feel myself collapse. It was then I realised they weren't chasing *me*...

Jenna Ashley Cooper (11)
The Roseland Academy, Tregony

The Rage

A sunny day, another day to leave my home and go to school. Turquoise-coloured flowers bloomed wildly as green grass moved swiftly with the not-so-powerful wind. Break and lunchtime bring me joy as my friends run around and play with me. Walking to my next lesson, saying, "Goodbye," to my friends, going to history, learning about humans. How strange they are. Climbing into our car, flying saucers fly around us rapidly, landing to collect my friends and fellow classmates! I am the last human left on Earth. The rage built and built slowly but surely.

Chloe Edwards (11)

The Roseland Academy, Tregony

No Escape

All of a sudden, it screamed and tiny footsteps got closer towards me. After paying respects to my passed-away father, that's when I saw it... Lurking behind a tree, it was watching my every move. I didn't pay attention to it, then it disappeared so I started walking to the exit. That's when I realised I was being followed. I heard a scream and ran, and repetitive footsteps followed behind me. I turned to look and there it was, right behind me, breathing very heavy. 'It' screamed again. I ran to the gate to leave. Oh no... it was locked!

Brody Gibson (13)
The Roseland Academy, Tregony

Specimen 3

For years, people have hunted animals.
"Door open!"
"What? No. Close door, now!"
He was ripped to parts for years. We've been trying to find this creature. We named it Specimen 3, until it was spotted on a radar. We ran and ran. It was massive, but something... about his eyes were calming, manipulative. They were saying, *come closer.* I knew I shouldn't, but it was dragging me. Captain went first, he ate him. No one responded, I snapped out of a spell but no one else did. Specimen 3 was a psycho, he didn't use his fists, only soul...

Brandon Garrett (11)
The Roseland Academy, Tregony

Whispers Of The Trees

With my face battered with mud, my rain-drenched legs stumbled forward. My eyes wearily dragged left and right, the trees becoming blurred and fuzzy before me. The flashlight circled above me, missing my head by inches. As I ran forward, eyes blundered by rain, random gunfire sputtered around me like confetti, nailing the trees with brutal force. Then it hit me. I felt the lead go through me, piercing my appendix before slamming into a tree. Air was punched out of me, oxygen scrabbling at my lungs. My legs buckled. I fell. My eyelids slid shut. I was dead.

Lochlainn Finn Lönze (11)
The Roseland Academy, Tregony

The Escape

Running. Every day I get reminded of that time, that day, that second. We didn't have much time, but it was a life or death situation; like a game of hide-and-seek. Soldiers like predators. Dogs like werewolves. Us like prey. Gasping for air, *bang.* Suddenly, time slowed down, running in slow motion. I could feel the cold air hitting my face and my short hair flying around. Then it hit him. A matter of seconds and his life was over. "Bruno! Bruno!" I was crying. I waved goodbye and his eyes closed. It was meant to be *me.*

Lily Miller (13)
The Roseland Academy, Tregony

Before They Found Us

Gasping for breath, we finally find shelter in a house, a forgotten fossil of the town's past. Rain thundering against the windows, we step inside, relieved. Protection from the storm at last. The musty smell lingers in the air as we tiptoe down hallways and in and out of rooms. Breaking the eerie silence, we hear footsteps upstairs. Have we disturbed the forgotten spirits? Our hearts racing, we turn to each other and question why we ever set foot in this dilapidated ruin of a house. We had been warned. That's when I knew we had to leave. Now!

Amelia Wykes (12)
The Roseland Academy, Tregony

Window

I peered out of my left-side window. I was 1000ft in the air, with the scorching sun beaming down on me. It was so peaceful. Then the pilot began clawing at his neck, gagging and choking. His face turned a deathly shade of grey, like the same colour as the now-bleak horizon. We began to descend, swerving left and right. The sky, which seconds before seemed so reliable, gave way. The night was black. Minutes, hours, days could have passed, however, an ominous feeling lingered in the air. A shriek echoed throughout me and then there was just darkness.

Toby Milnes (12)
The Roseland Academy, Tregony

The Hunt

I couldn't run for much longer. It was becoming harder to breathe every step that I took. I was running blindly into the foggy forest, not knowing if I'd survive the hunt. I could hear sinister screams coming from every direction. Was I next? I felt helpless as I ran into the unknown. Sirens were wailing, leaves were crunching and people were screaming. What now? I could hear them coming closer. My heart beating heroically in my chest, I stopped but only for a few seconds, until I heard nothing, just silence. Was it over? Did I win the hunt?

Zenna Martin (12)
The Roseland Academy, Tregony

Hunted

The sirens' wail echoed through the forest. They were close. I ran as fast as I could. I didn't mean to do it. It was an accident. A little white lie which blew out of proportion. The dead autumn leaves crunched as my feet hit the ground. The sun gradually became darker. The owls were starting to come alive. The cold breeze hit my face as the sirens' wail stopped unexpectedly. I slowly turned around. To my horror, standing there in a black suit, was my father.
"What have you done?" came a voice from the back of a tree...

Sophie Kent (12)
The Roseland Academy, Tregony

Blood On The Horizon

Alec had run his whole life. Staying still was a death sentence and, though his life was dreadful, it was all he had left. It had to be close, it had nearly caught him earlier. He surveyed the area, the brick and dirt of an alley. A low rasping noise sounded behind him. Oh gods, it was here. Swift and soulless, it crept towards him, white teeth glistening in the moonlight. Alec's heart felt like it was about to burst from his chest! It hissed once more. Something clicked. It wanted something. He didn't know what. This was absolutely awful.

Jemima Hetherington (12)
The Roseland Academy, Tregony

The Labyrinth

Emily ran. She didn't dare look back. She turned the corner. There it was, the final piece. She grabbed it and laughed. She finally had it! Emily turned, what was that? There was the beast, its eyes gleaming and its long metallic claws scraping against the wall. Emily grinned, she slammed the piece into the blade. It glowed like a thousand suns and it fused into a weapon. Emly yelled as she charged at the beast, it was startled as this has never happened before. But it was too late; Emily sliced the beast in half. She defeated the labyrinth.

Harry Gildersleeve (12)
The Roseland Academy, Tregony

Don't Look In The Mirror...

You can't see me. You can't hear me. But I'm always here. I stalk through your dreams, your nightmares, even your memories. You don't know who you are. But I do. The thing is, I killed you. I killed you a long time ago. Bet that surprised you, ha! Why do you think you got lost in the darkness? Anyway, I needed you. It was only for a little while, just for me to... let's call it 'fulfil' my needs. But you would not comply. You refused.
I'm back now. And I'm coming. Don't blame me. You used the mirror.

Sarah Mitchell (12)
The Roseland Academy, Tregony

Are They Here Yet?

The siren started. We had to hide, but it was too dark to see anything at all.

"Are they here yet?" my brother whispered.

"Shh! They'll hear us!" I said, petrified. But it was too late... They were normally very loud coming up the stairs. But this time, they caught us. We knew they heard us from the unearthly scream that came from one of them. The door came crashing down. I saw unhuman feet. They were slimy, it was like an alien. In a split second, the creature put its ear to the floor, facing me. It saw me...

Lily Rose Boboefe (12)
The Roseland Academy, Tregony

One Child's Death

It wasn't a human. It couldn't be. It was twice the size of me. My gut instinct was, make a run for it, so I did. I was now hiding behind a collapsed boulder, watching volcanic lava erupting from the horizon. My heart was beating faster than it ever had before. I had until the sun set till I would fall to my death... *Crash!* There it was. *Crash!* There it was again. The creature scraped its hand across a metal container, making a deafening sound fill the air. Step by step, the figure came closer and closer towards me...

Charlie Wheeler

The Roseland Academy, Tregony

The Gate

Blood dripped from my eyebrow and collected in my eyelashes, blurring my vision. Illuminating the towering timber trees laid in front of me, the moon rose from the clouds. Any other day, I would have seen this as magical, but not today. Not now. My own panting rang in my ears as my feet pounded the earth, every step sending agony into my bones. Aching. Bleeding. Eventually, I would have to stop. Wheezing for breath, I heard the moans grow louder. It wouldn't stop. My mind was buzzing with anxiety as the gate came into view. I'm almost safe...

Amelia Harrington (12)
The Roseland Academy, Tregony

Running

I'm running, running as fast and as far as my legs can take me. I don't think that could be much longer. I can hear it behind me. The leaves crunching under its feet. My heart is racing, pounding against my ribcage. I look around. Scanning the area around me. I crouch behind a tree, hoping that whatever it is would get lost in the woods. Gasping for air, I remind myself that there's something still out there. Watching me, waiting to pounce. The silence reverberates, filling me with dread, filling me with horror. It's not safe.

Skyeanne Nash (13)

The Roseland Academy, Tregony

Playing With Fire

My heart dances in my chest. A blood-curdling scream fills the air, making the hairs on my arm stand on end. It takes me minutes to realise that it's coming from me. I clamp my mouth shut, my laboured breathing increases, my temperature plummets. My blood freezes, fire crackles at my fingertips. A door opens and I'm roughly dragged into a bright white room. I let out a shaky breath, smiling slightly. It's over. I take in my surroundings, I have to leave. My hands burn as I hold them out in front of me. Alarms scream. Time to run.

Lily Jones (12)
The Roseland Academy, Tregony

The School Intruder

I was sat in English when this alarm went off that nobody had ever heard before. We were all confused. Eyes were wide. I heard one boy shout, "What's that?"
I heard the teacher inform the whole class, "There's an intruder." So we all hid under the desks. In the cupboard. The door was locked. A shadow of what looked to be a person swiftly walked past the door. As if he knew his way around the school already. I managed to get access to the school's CCTV. What I saw was horrifying. It was the headmaster...

Adam Clow (13)
The Roseland Academy, Tregony

The Virus

Somewhere in a facility underground, experiments were being done for a virus that they named 'The Noli Virus'. This was a really aggressive substance. One fateful day, it escaped. The effects of the Noli Virus were that it would form into a mask of sadness and the body of the host got drenched in the substance, and it bonded to it. When it reached 6,999,999,999 people, it was unstoppable! But then someone managed to extract the virus. He had to go to every country until all of it was gone. Then they found a way to destroy it...

Alfie Alexander Heslip (12)
The Roseland Academy, Tregony

The Raven Of Sorrow

The wind was howling, rain was pouring. I ran. A raven followed. The tall imposing trees blocked my path, standing like evil custodians. It stood on crimson rocks, singing an evil song. It flew near me. It perched on my arm, eating chunks of flesh. Blood bled, its oversized talons cutting me like paper. What could I do? I was cornered. My arm was torn, the soil blood-red. In my velvet pocket was a knife. I grabbed it. I stabbed the silver blade into the creature's brain. It laid on the floor, twitching and dead. Gone. Never again.

Thomas Edwards (11)

The Roseland Academy, Tregony

The Chase

We have to leave. Now. I could feel their breath down my back, closer every second. We ran for our lives. I was out of breath, but I didn't care, I kept going, didn't stop. Gunshots fired over our heads. We ran through a dark alleyway with narrow walls brushing against my shoulders. Why we were on a chase, I didn't know. Who they were, I didn't know. All I knew was that they were after us and we needed to get away. And quickly. Faster and faster they were pursuing us. They wouldn't stop until they had destroyed us.

Yumi Storey (12)
The Roseland Academy, Tregony

Hunted

The sirens wailed, I had to escape. I had to get away from the asylum, from everything. I ran as fast as I could until my legs burnt and ached. I could still hear the sirens wailing and guard shouting. I slipped down a muddy slope into a garden - well, I thought it was a garden. I kept drifting in and out of consciousness.

A while later, I stood up and found myself in a shed. *Where am I?* I thought. *Who brought me here?* Was I in the asylum? I shouted, "Is anyone there?" and a shadow appeared outside...

Fia Brunton (11)
The Roseland Academy, Tregony

The Game

The game. Harmless. Promises he could never keep. For the first time in days, the door opened and he stood there; his body hung above me. His words merged into one, my brain was delirious. Before I could stop myself, my legs started running. I was free but trapped forever. Thoughts ran through my head, one by one, slowly tearing me down. The game. Harmless.

I saw them. The red handkerchiefs hung on trees. He gave them to us as tokens of life, but all he gave us were really tokens of death. I turned around and expected my fate...

Olivia Rees-Challis (12)
The Roseland Academy, Tregony

Hunted Fox

I could hear leaves crunching, getting louder every step. I'm a lonely fox, trying to run away from a hunter. I started to hear loud noises. *Bang! Bang!* They were gun noises. I started running away from the hunter as he started getting closer and closer. The hunter was killing other innocent animals at the same time and quickly picked them up and put them in his big dirty bag. The hunter pulled back the rusty trigger and the cold bullet hit the back of my head. I was quickly put in the dirty bag and slowly closed my eyes.

Daisy Thomas (12)
The Roseland Academy, Tregony

Twenty-Four Hours

I had twenty-four hours. I needed to act quick! I gathered up my bags and got hunting. The horse went missing yesterday when the clock struck twelve. I didn't know why this was. The only evidence we have is the footprints outside Stormy's box. I knew I never should have left her outside overnight with the dodgy padlock! This has been the biggest regret of my life. I gazed up into the clouds. With that, I heard Stormy's neigh, and all of a sudden the clouds began to part. I smiled, she was brought to me, she was home.

Phoebe Sophia Emmett (12)

The Roseland Academy, Tregony

Run!

The exit was blocked, I had to go down to the next floor, using the elevator shaft. I made it down to the fourth floor but no one was there. I had to find a working phone somewhere, but where? I could see the flashing lights from outside, but as the fire raged on, my chances of survival were lowering. Suddenly, a shadow emerged from the burning flames, making its way towards me. I froze in fear, I couldn't think. I clambered into the nearest cupboard and hid for my life. The cupboard door creaked, an eerie voice said, "Hello..."

Theo Schofield (13)
The Roseland Academy, Tregony

An Unknown Man, An Unknown Number

I had just woken up from what felt like a nightmare. I got out of bed and it was around 10:30 in the morning. My parents weren't home, no one was. I felt petrified.

Later on that day, at 1:40, here was a police chase just down the lane. I was walking, I went down a dark alleyway. In front of me was a petrifying figure. Suddenly, the police ran towards me with pistols! I was worried, I haven't done anything wrong!

Later on that day, I got a text from an unknown number. It said 'Nice seeing you today'...

Callum Knight (14)
The Roseland Academy, Tregony

The Forbidden Wood

Sirens wailed, we couldn't stop. We were fastened stuck, cornered. The only way to go was into the forbidden wood. No one ever made it out. We had no choice. Running through the beguiling trees, finally able to stop and take a break, panting, struggling to breathe, we had no track of time and all we knew was we could no longer see what was ahead of us. Hiding in a cave, we heard petrifying noises coming from outside, but they weren't ordinary. The animals of the day were scared of me, but currently I'm the prey...

Maddi Sophia Kent-Fuller (13)
The Roseland Academy, Tregony

The Well

I couldn't run for much longer; the hunt was on. Sprinting, panic drove me. Towering above me, the trees slept in the dark void. Falling, falling to my death. Where was I? In pain, I attempted to stand. My future inevitably led to death. My feet were soaking. Water was flooding in through a pipe. I couldn't swim. As I tried to climb out, I twisted my ankle. The water rose, above my ankles, onto my knees, to my hips. Shivers slid down my spine. Death was awaiting me. Sitting in my grave. Waiting for the perfect time to strike.

Megan Richards (12)
The Roseland Academy, Tregony

The Final Encounter

I couldn't run for much longer; surely they'll find me soon. It's only a matter of minutes before... it... finds us. All we can do is have hope, hope in the force to guide us to safety, away from the Dark Lord. He has cameras, way too many, and they're everywhere. There's no escape and his lasers will be fired soon. His lasers can destroy whole planets, Teacat is his next target... We're doomed to die! I must hide wherever I can, quick! Prepare the lightsabers, a war is coming, the war to end all wars. I must participate...

Chloe Enfield (12)
The Roseland Academy, Tregony

Hide, Actually Run!

Find a hiding spot! Crouch? Kneel? Balance? Whatever... just hide! We chose a bin, that's all we could find. I hid behind, Mia hid in it and Michelle was next to the side. What have we done? Sirens started to wail. Flashbacks came to my head of what I have done in the past. Why this time of the day? I went light-headed. The ringing sound was getting closer. My ears felt like they were going to explode any moment. I regretted all of this. Get out now. Now! Run for your life. Police dogs charged.
"You're now arrested."

Macey Rodda (11)
The Roseland Academy, Tregony

Guess Who?

A game, they said. Harmless. Just for fun. Really? I was innocent, yet they were still out there. They had the weapon; I had moments left to live. Five gunshots went off, followed by a piercing scream. There they were. I knew who it was. It was over when they were dead, or we were all dead. Black boots, a blood-covered shirt, and a loaded gun. I sneezed. They heard. But, at that moment, I realised it wasn't a person. This wasn't an innocent game, it was all a big trick, and I wasn't coming out of here alive...

Bethany Champion (12)
The Roseland Academy, Tregony

On The Run

I regret this. I had twenty-four hours, helicopters and snipers in the back. I heard a shout, "Ready for take-off!" I ran in the woods, I saw huskies and a sleigh attached. I hopped on, then got the ropes and started to drive. I heard the helicopters swooping behind, police sirens all behind. I thought to myself, *should I pull over, admit what I did, or make it worse and carry on?* I said, "Never." I carried on going as fast as light. They sped up to try to get in front, but I sped more. They said, "Stop, now!"

Alfie Lambirth (11)
The Roseland Academy, Tregony

Run

We have to leave. Now! We were running, running for our lives. We were stuck. The room was small, dark and cold. We were hiding, I could hear it. It was coming, coming for us. Hunting, hunting for blood, fresh blood. Our blood. The ground was shaking, I could hear the crashing of furniture falling to the ground. Light... I could see light. It was a bad kind of light; a bright light coming from the door. The bolt had come undone, we were doomed. It got her. She was... she was dead. Tears streaming down, I had to run...

Niamh Star Burnett (13)
The Roseland Academy, Tregony

Peek-A-Boo

Every second felt like an hour. I knew she wanted me dead. "Let's play hide-and-seek," she called out songfully. I couldn't breathe as I tried to run away, but there was no escape. There was a creepy doll in a haunted house, trying to hunt me down. I found a place to hide and my life flashed before my eyes. My childhood nightmare was becoming a reality. I heard her murderous voice call my name, so I ran into another room, but she was sat in the rocking chair, staring at me.

"Peek-A-Boo!" She had found me...

Sophia Tame (13)

The Roseland Academy, Tregony

The Miniature Monkey

Just like every other Friday night, my son James and I were out hunting in the fun forest, although it was covered in darkness. What I didn't know was the miniature monkeys were out (the most dangerous animal in world), plotting to tickle every living soul in the world. In the canopy, I could see the blue body of a miniature monkey. The arms were twice the size of its body (which wasn't very long), leaping from treetop to treetop. I looked over to see James to make sure he was still there. He was a miniature monkey!

Lucas Burton (12)
The Roseland Academy, Tregony

156

Werewolf

I am a freak. I have no friends because I am a werewolf! Soldiers are always after me, to experiment on me, but I always survive. Me and my brother were running from the soldiers until John pushed me over and I was almost caught, but I slaughtered all of them. After that, I found my brother and I said, "Why would you do that?"
He replied, "Because I hate you! You're always hurting me and taking my food. And so now you die!"
I realised that I had stabbed into my brother's chest.
"I am sorry, brother."

Jacob White (13)
The Roseland Academy, Tregony

Snap

I could hear the gunshots. My heart ached and hurt, but I kept on running. Branches scratched my skin. My head throbbed, I climbed up the rocks, my hooves slipped but to keep my life I had to keep on going. I had so much left to do, I wanted to stop running but I knew if I did, the bloodthirsty silver-eyed men would catch me. My legs stung, it felt like tiny needles stabbing me every minute, every second. My antlers snapped the branches above me. *Bang!* I felt a sharp strong pain, then I fell to the ground.

Caera Dye (11)
The Roseland Academy, Tregony

Am I In A Dream?

All around me were trees and greenery. Where was I? The smell around me smelt familiar, it had a fruity citrus scent, just like my mother's perfume. I started shouting, "Mother, Mother!" I could hear a door open but I was in the middle of a forest. How was this happening? A whisper of my name echoed through my head, making me stumble to the ground. It was soft. It felt like my bed. I could hear my mum's calming voice whirling through my head. Suddenly, my eyes flickered and I could see my old room again. I'm alive!

Ella Wheildon (11)
The Roseland Academy, Tregony

The Runaway Queen

Crystal-blue eyes closed, but there were transparent tears. Turning my head, my raven flew in my face. I rode on with the man that would save him. He screamed my name, begging me to come back. No; I had chosen my path. I'm going to save him, no matter what. We approached a sheer drop, they had found us. It all happened so fast, but he grabbed my arm and pulled me in. Air rushed past me, icy water surrounded me. My lungs filled with frosty water. Then I saw it. His expressionless face met my eyes and never left.

Keala Harrington (12)
The Roseland Academy, Tregony

The Chase

Running. Terrified. Hunted. I darted between the long grass and my eyes zoomed like the rockets full of thoughts in my head. My heart was beating in my throat and I didn't dare look behind me. The forest was just ahead. I decided to focus on the intricate arrangement of flowers. My feet whipped the ground like it was cake mix. My toes sank into the mud and it flicked up again (the mud was no match for the tiny feet of my pursuer). I leapt into my home, my little beloved rabbit hole. Rabbit and fox. I am hunted.

Matilda Rose Park (13)
The Roseland Academy, Tregony

The Apocalypse

All of a sudden, I saw its grotesque pus-covered face and it lunged towards me. I stepped out of its path and tried to hit it with my club. I missed and ran out of the dark alley, into the street. It was oddly quiet in the street. Almost too quiet. The zombies had always chased me, but they seemed like they were smarter than usual. The one that attacked me back in the alley had ambushed me. They normally just limped out and hopped towards you, groaning. Then I heard it coming towards me again. I was being hunted.

Christopher Harris (12)
The Roseland Academy, Tregony

The Prey

We were in a nightmare. We were hunted, but so were they. The tower blocks made it harder to see who was following us. Panic was driving us towards the vast open fields. Everywhere was dead ends with the winding city streets, the only place to go was the fields. We all stopped, the group behind crashed into us like waves against a harbour. The sirens were wailing and some of the people around me were too. My throat felt like it was on fire. They had caught us, but we were the predator, not the prey. We're Hunted.

Stella McNeill (12)

The Roseland Academy, Tregony

Zombie

I had to leave, just had to. These things, 'zombies', ate everyone I knew and cared about, and they were coming for me now. *Groan!* I could hear the zombies catching up with me. I ran faster, my pistol digging into my thighs. Suddenly, I lost my footing and fell over. My leg was in agony and, try as I might, I couldn't get up. The zombies were slowly making their way towards me. Eventually, I got up and started to limp my way out of harm's way. But my legs failed me and the zombies caught up once again...

Alfie Young (13)
The Roseland Academy, Tregony

The Mystery

The sirens wailed as they tried to find them. Everyone around me scared, terrified to say the least. Everyone was calling their kids names as they all scattered like mice trying to run from a cat. All of us knew we wouldn't make it, and we had to say goodbye. The blood poured everywhere the eye could see. It seemed as if we were in a maze with no exit or middle. We were all trapped... Everyone seemed to be running from the police. It was then we saw... strange dots in the sky, looking for me. *Bang!*

Erin Richards (12)
The Roseland Academy, Tregony

On The Run

I was in the forest. I could hear shouts, I knew they were close. I was crouching behind an old log. I could see the light from their torch getting closer and closer. I peeked over the log and *bam!* All I remember seeing was a fist go into my face. They put me in handcuffs and dragged me to their car. I regained consciousness and realised there was the only one in the back, so I kicked his hand, he spun out and the window smashed while the chain slipped on my hand. But then someone grabbed my hand...

Louie Maddern (11)
The Roseland Academy, Tregony

Spy

It was all happening. Someone appeared at my window, so I ran to shut the curtains. I had a spy on my street. I was home alone, with no electric or food, so I entertained myself. Until a person at my window again. Right there. Thoughts racing, *why me?*

Knock, knock, knock. I did not answer. It was 12am. There was a bang on the window, it was my parents! I was relieved. I let them in and worries were lifted. I was happy. No longer alone. I sat down with my parents and ate our tasty tea!

Sophie Perryman (11)
The Roseland Academy, Tregony

The Escape To Freedom

I could not run for much longer; my feet were as red as blood, or were they covered in blood? My hands were tied down. We all kept going for it was die from a bullet or die from starvation. I was frightened. 500 children were on the run for freedom. My limbs killed, feet swollen, blood dripped from my arm. Although I was seven when I got taken away from my parents, I faced many years. I could not see clearly what the future would be. I could hear them coming. The last breath I drew, then... *bang!*

Zoe Bodfish (12)
The Roseland Academy, Tregony

Dead End

Stuck. Nowhere to go. Where could I go? Sirens going off around me, where are they coming from? I look around, only to see darkness creep up on me. Bodies. There are bodies! Have people been here before me? I must come out of here alive, but that might not even be possible. Praying for my life, I frantically run around corners, only to find one dead end leading to another dead end, leading to another. Nowhere I go lets me get out free. "I'm innocent!" I shout, but all I hear is an echo reply back to me...

Isla Harvey (12)
The Roseland Academy, Tregony

The Werewolf Girl

It's not safe now they know... that I'm a werewolf. So right now, I'm running away because I have twenty-four hours to live. Then, all of a sudden, there was lightning. *Crash, crash, crash, boom, boom, boom!* It was only the start. Now the police are trying to find me, so I must transform to a... lost pet. But they still know, so I must keep running away for my life. But the sun is rising and I must disappear...
To find out that I was asleep all along! I woke up as a... werewolf!

Kara Clarke (12)
The Roseland Academy, Tregony

The Predator

We had to leave. Now! It was coming. I knew it, we all did. The noise in the background got closer and closer, the claws scraping the ground. Then we heard it. There was a scream. I looked behind me, I knew I shouldn't but I did and it was awful... My friend was on the floor in agony, crying, screaming. The creature was closer, just around the corner. It came around the corner, it was not what we thought it was. It had big round eyes...
It was a small lost puppy with eyes that looked right into you!

Iona Moran (13)
The Roseland Academy, Tregony

Darkness

Darkness. You couldn't see. The air was suffocating. I crouched in the corner of the room, watching the malicious red flashing light illuminating the room. The room was tiny and surely I would be found, for the room was like a sieve and I was the last grain of sand. Time was nearly up and I had to find a way to escape, fast. My hot breath clung to the metal around me, hiding from the hunter. I reached into my pocket and pulled out my silver blade. If I was going down, I was going down with a fight...

Zac H Humphreys (12)
The Roseland Academy, Tregony

Predator And Prey

We had to leave that second; I could feel something behind us, the same feeling I had had for miles. I looked behind me, nothing but trees. I looked in front of me and everyone else had disappeared. I screamed and ran. Everywhere I looked there was what seemed like a rabid wolf. I thought it was just me imagining things, until I heard what sounded like barking, but sort of human. I turned around and it was like my friends in wolf form! I felt a breath on my shoulder, the predator was there to kill me...

Jacob Parr (11)
The Roseland Academy, Tregony

Crimson Waters

He ran, stumbling on rocks and small bushes. He startled himself on a small murder of crows nesting in the trees. This... thing was chasing him, she had superhuman strength and the vision of thirty mountain hawks. She had swords that trapped the souls of victims. He could see the river, it was a sin to swim in the pool, even if you dared to dip your fingertip into it, your soul would be torn into eight bodies living cursed lives in agony. He had no choice; Jay dived in. He felt searing pain, then death.

Evie Hepworth (13)
The Roseland Academy, Tregony

Trapped

I had twenty-four hours. Twenty-four hours to leave, escape and run away. I always thought of running away when I was younger, but now I wish I could stay and not leave my childhood home. I couldn't run for much longer. My legs were aching, my stomach was churning, I didn't know if I could make it. But I had to keep going.

I stopped, glancing around every corner. It was a dead end. I spotted a wall, it was small and easy to climb. I got up and jumped over. I landed in someone's arms. They got me!

Pip Richards (11)
The Roseland Academy, Tregony

The Hunted

My life is over! I don't know why life is worth living no more. This older-looking lady walked up to me, walking with a very fast pace, almost marching. She startled me, I fell, all I could see was darkness. Then the older-looking lady said something I didn't think was true...
I heard the sirens wail, I needed to run and fast or I would be dead. This time, I ran as fast as my legs would carry me. It felt like I was flying, nearly. This is my nightmare. Always has been. In fact, always will be...

Elowyn Floyd-Norris (11)
The Roseland Academy, Tregony

Face-To-Face With A Predator

Suddenly, I was running. Not from a human but a predator. It was fast. Very fast. The creature had razor-sharp black claws and beady red eyes. My heart started pounding so fast I could feel my chest move. I stopped and took cover behind a tree. I could hear it sniffing the air. It could smell me but not see me. I couldn't run, breathe, move. I was being handed to the creature on a plate. It stepped towards me. I had to run now! I picked up a rock and took a gulp of air, chucking the rock away...

Jake Kingsley-Heath (11)
The Roseland Academy, Tregony

Tag

I couldn't run for much longer. The screams wailed louder and louder as I sprinted for my life. My lungs were screaming for me to take a breath... but it was too late now. I ran and ran until it was impossible to take one more step. I looked around, I was safe. Before I could take one more step, I was pushed. My heart pounding, my head dizzy, trousers covered in mud, this was it. I had been caught. I looked at this girl to see her laughing. She looked me in the eye and screamed, "Tag!"

Ruby Tuesday Laura Bullock (12)

The Roseland Academy, Tregony

Just The Beginning

My legs were tired, my heart pounding, but I kept going. I felt like I had been running for hours. I couldn't slow down, I wanted to stop but I could hear sirens, I could see the lights! I looked around, I didn't know where I was, but I saw something move. It looked monstrous. I stared at it for a second but it started moving, running right towards me, its feet pounding. I could see its face, it was terrifying, it was unreal! I ran faster, then it happened. It was here. It started. I am the hunted.

Hope Smith (12)
The Roseland Academy, Tregony

Picnic Peril

Me and my younger sister went to go have a picnic in the woods. She suggested we play hide-and-seek. I counted, she ran and hid. I finished counting and I started to look for her. I couldn't find her. The minutes turned into hours. I screamed her name, no one replied. Then an older-looking lady came and told me she would take me home. She drove straight past my house to an abandoned house. She tied me up to a chair, picked up a glass of poison and drank it in front of me and died! Would I survive?

Natalie Mitchell (11)
The Roseland Academy, Tregony

The Chase!

It was a cold crisp night. I was perched on a tree. It was not safe. I had twenty-four hours to keep hidden. I heard a motorcycle zoom past me, I was waddling for my life to the rotten overgrown forest. I climbed up a tree, they found me hopping from one tree to another. Shooting bullets, they got me in the tail! My beady eyes planned on getting to a cave where no one would find me. I failed my quest, poachers shot me, the pheasant, right in the stomach. My beak hit the ground. Thoughts were gone.

Poppy Miller (11)
The Roseland Academy, Tregony

The Chase

I had twenty-four hours. I had been picked for 'The Chase', a game show for the upper tiers, where sixty of us were caught and killed. The first siren sounded and we ran, others had made alliances but I hadn't, so I was alone. I had already make it to the edge of the forest when the second siren sounded. Gunshots followed and the boy next to me collapsed to the forest floor, but I had almost won this. As it turns out, I had outrun most of the rest. Thirty of us entered and one left...

Piran Spackman (12)

The Roseland Academy, Tregony

Phone Calls

It was every night I had these phone calls, but then it started happening every hour. They would say stuff like, "I can see you." "You don't have long." "Say your goodbyes." It was starting to get weird. I would tell people but then something bad would happen to me, so I don't tell anyone anymore. I decided to go an find them. I looked up their phone number and tracked them down. They were in the woods, they found me. I ran, it was too late. I was shot to the floor, left to bleed to death. Help!

Isla Clode (11)
The Roseland Academy, Tregony

Running For Freedom

I looked at him dead on the floor, blood dripping from his head. He was so close to making it with me. But he was a true friend and he would want me to carry on, so I did. I ran... I could hear the sound of police sirens nearing me from behind, so I quickly increased my pace and leapt up onto a 5ft fence. The razor-sharp spikes on the fence cut deep into my bitter cold hands. I jumped down with blood dripping from my hands. Suddenly, a bullet was shot. *Bang!* I fell to the ground.

Jack Oscar Ellis (12)
The Roseland Academy, Tregony

The School Trip

Being the ten-year-old I was, I didn't know any better. It was just a school trip. What could go wrong? We snuck up behind the trees in the forest. They counted our heads for the twelfth time. Of course, me and my friend hadn't thought it through. What would we do? We could set up a den with the materials around us, we could fly away in a plane we found hidden by the bushes. Although all of those thoughts went away in a second. There was a wolf! It sprinted towards me. I screamed!

Rowan Goostrey (11)
The Roseland Academy, Tregony

The Cold-Hearted Vampire

It's not safe now they know what I am. This is a nightmare. I want to move and never see this place again. People screaming, shouting because their loved ones have died. Because of me! I am a cold-hearted vampire. I loved being a vampire, but when I came back, I met a boy. He was the love of my life. I turned him into a vampire. Worst mistake of my life. He was horrible, he tried to kill me and my friends. I had to kill him. That's why I am running, because they know what I am...

Hettie Brown (12)
The Roseland Academy, Tregony

What I Saw

We went to my friend's house to play hide-and-seek. I was seeking, everyone else was hiding. I searched everywhere, but I could find no one. Ten minutes later, still no one. I was beginning to wonder if they were all playing a nasty trick on me. They do that sometimes. When I looked in the wardrobe, I found something I will never forget in my life. I ran away from the house and even past my house. I ran as far as I could. I try to never think about it. I wish it was a normal day...

Sam Hitchens (13)
The Roseland Academy, Tregony

The Ghost

I left that life behind, now it had come back to haunt me. Literally. A figure was floating towards me, it had a vaguely human shape, it was like it absorbed all light and happiness. I was running as fast as possible. I saw a stick, I threw it at it. It went through and out it emerged a pile of ashes. As it moved, all lights went off and it grew darker and more defined, then black tendrils came flying at me. I barely avoided them and then one hit me, flying towards me. I screamed...

Henry Myles (12)

The Roseland Academy, Tregony

Twenty-Four Hours

I had twenty-four hours until the hunt finished - I had to be quick or I'd run out of time. I watched everyone run when the bell rang to go! I was scared, but I was also excited. I knew I had five minutes until the next siren, this is when they would release the animal. Nobody knew what it was. I hardly had any time to run and hide. Then, suddenly, they let it out! The siren went and we were all terrified. I ran and ran as fast as I could. I found my first clue - I was lost...

Ileana Eleni Karsa (11)
The Roseland Academy, Tregony

The Nightmare

I couldn't run for much longer, since I knew the police were onto me. I had to place the body on the ground somewhere for two reasons. Reason one: it looked like the person tripped and fell. Reason two: it was very heavy. Everywhere I ran, in the back of my head I heard the sirens wailing. It's not that safe now; I know it's not. I tell myself I have to wake up. I have to. I yell out for my parents to come and tell me it's okay. I realise it was all a perfect dreadful nightmare!

Ava Mallett (12)
The Roseland Academy, Tregony

Street Flee

I ran for what seemed to be multiple days, and still, the uniformed people chased me. My legs were giving in, but I had to keep going. I had seen the adverts. I had seen the flames. All I had been told was a lie. And now the uniformed man wanted me dead. The train my friends were on wasn't leaving, so I thought they only wanted me. I had run through all the streets I knew, and yet the people were still coming after a kid. Now I'm writing on a scrap of paper I found on the floor.

Jacob Allen (12)
The Roseland Academy, Tregony

Hide-And-Seek

We all started hiding. The boys hid separately but the girls hid together. It was now half an hour into the game. Seven people had been found, there were three to go. An hour went, one more found. There were now two people left to find, it was getting dark as well. 11pm, it was really hard to see. No one else found. 11:47pm, it was pitch-black and the only place not checked was the old barn. They came in. Creaks and cracks found their way to us. We gave up and finally came out.

Jacob Taylor-McHale (12)
The Roseland Academy, Tregony

In The Running...

I was in the running to be hunted. It's all a game... or so I thought. You would have to run from... it. The ghost of death, the woman in white, she would come to find you and never leave, never. How you got picked was simple; you had to run and hide. No child was allowed to enter, ever. You had to be the toughest in the world. "Run!" they would say, you'd have to run and not get taken by the woman in white. She would say, "Come with me." Everyone else said, "Okay." I'm hunted.

Ysabelle Iles (12)
The Roseland Academy, Tregony

Ghost Hunter

How did I get here? It all started when I was asleep and the electricity went and the doorbell rang. I got up, I went to the door, I could see an outline of a person. I ran away, they opened the door. I went from door to door, I went to the bathroom and I locked the door. The thing went through the bottom of the door. I unlocked the door and ran to bed. I went to sleep.

I went to the doctors the next day. He checked me out, he said to me, "You can see ghosts!"

Ollie Budge (11)
The Roseland Academy, Tregony

The Death Sentence

They knew I couldn't run for much longer. I panicked and tried to run, but when I tried to escape I realised that the entrance was a dead end. They were catching up with me. I needed to hide. I hid behind a bush and tried not to make a sound, but they knew I was there so I distracted them with a stone and made a run for it. They noticed I had left. I didn't know how many of them there were. Then I saw! It was like I was on a radar. I was being hunted...

Elik Olivia Poole (12)
The Roseland Academy, Tregony

Running

I have twenty-four hours to leave, else it will be here waiting for me. I am the prey. Something somewhere is watching me. I don't know how but I will find a way to disappear. I am running, running for my life. It knows where I was, where I am and where I am going. It's after me and I don't know what to do. I'm trapped, scared of the world around me. I need help and I don't know who to trust or where is safe. I am being hunted. I'm alone and frightened...

Erin Ward (13)
The Roseland Academy, Tregony

The Hunt

It was coming. I couldn't stop now! I knew it was coming for me. Where would I go? What would I do? There were footsteps. Closer... Closer... Closer! There was only one way out - the window! My hands were shaking as I reached for the lock. My head throbbed as I clambered onto the windowsill. Once I reached the ground, I knew I just had to run. But it was too late. I was surrounded...

Jodie Wyatt (11)
The Roseland Academy, Tregony

Belly Ache

The cries melted into a high-pitched ring; my favourite Billie Eilish song on repeat in my brain. Behind me, monsters stalked me, wanting to devour my tender flesh. They were hunting me. The deceased laid lifeless, their souls lifted lightly from their carcasses, the lives I stole. I wasn't immune to the pain anymore; I had given in. I was hunted, and now I have a belly ache.

Ruby-June Grunberger-Miles (12)
The Roseland Academy, Tregony

The Problem With Magic

An electrifying howl rippled across the beach. They were gaining. Over my shoulder, I saw their small, sleek bodies emerging over the ridge of stones. I raced on, past the sea troll's footprint. Now I wished I'd never found out what it was; I wished I had never discovered the magic. Suddenly, I stumbled and fell, sprawling over the cold sand. The Sea Gremlins and Raftors gathered in a circle before me. I backed away from them, my breath pounding raggedly until, suddenly, a dark shadow fell over me. I stared up into the sharp teeth of a demon crab...

Tommy Burrows (12)
West Buckland School, West Buckland

Exposed!

I couldn't run for much longer. Hills running in rows, rivers trickling through. The only sound I could hear was my breath. My eyes were like an owl's, wide open. Heart beating fast... *bang!* The sound of a gunshot. Running into the distant forest, echoing. They were still attacking like hungry wolves, pounding for their prey. My mind was running around, confused. I no longer knew if this was a dream or if this was my chance. I couldn't run. I had to hide, no time to spare. Night was caving in. This was my end.

Daisy Whelan (11)
West Buckland School, West Buckland

Dinner

They were gaining on me. "Give me starchy flesh!" they yelled menacingly. I attempted to jump the gate, but splatted with a squish against it. I turned to see an evil vegan grin on the Irish man chasing me, pitchfork and torch in hand. He caught me, starch bubbling. I tried to escape him, but before I knew it, I was a potato roasting on an open fire. I watched my potato family crying sorrowfully at home. As I watched them weeping, I decided to haunt the man who had cooked me, turning me into the dreaded ghost potato...

Isaac Spear (12)
West Buckland School, West Buckland

Tim The Tortoise

He was gaining on me. The roar of the engine was just behind me. I turned to see the carnivorous sheep at the wheel, his grin malicious and cruel. My memories flashed before my eyes. My mass world domination and my new claim to Footland. But, as if a light was switched off, I was brought back to reality. The combine harvester was just behind me. I knew I only had seconds left. My tortoise shell began crushing under the wheels. This was it. The sheep let out an evil cackle. This was the end of me, Tim the tortoise.

Isabella Watts (13)
West Buckland School, West Buckland

Taking Away The Badness

I was close; the wind felt as if it was pushing me back towards the blue and red dragons. They were gigantic, with eyes of wisdom and imagination, and teeth of shiny gold that resembled goodness and purity in the heart. All across my body laid guilt and fear, and these beasts were coming to feast upon my badness and leave only goodness in my body. But I kept running, as if my acts of wickedness couldn't be resolved with any form of goodness. I then stopped and I confronted my fears.
I felt peace at last.

Vincent Burton (12)
West Buckland School, West Buckland

YOUNG WRITERS INFORMATION

We hope you have enjoyed reading this book – and that you will continue to in the coming years.

If you're a young writer who enjoys reading and creative writing, or the parent of an enthusiastic poet or story writer, do visit our website **www.youngwriters.co.uk**. Here you will find free competitions, workshops and games, as well as recommended reads, a poetry glossary and our blog. There's lots to keep budding writers motivated to write!

If you would like to order further copies of this book, or any of our other titles, then please give us a call or order via your online account.

Young Writers
Remus House
Coltsfoot Drive
Peterborough
PE2 9BF
(01733) 890066
info@youngwriters.co.uk